THE BAILEY NOVELLAS

PIPER RAYNE

Operation Bailey Wedding (The Baileys #3.5)

BUZZ WHEEL PRESS RELEASE: No one could have guessed a marriage could sprout from a one-night stand, but Holly Radcliffe and Austin Bailey appear to be written in the stars. From the backseat of Austin's Jeep to the altar they go. Our entire town has been prepping for the event of the year, but as usual things never go smoothly. If you have the inside scoop on any of it be sure to let me know!

Operation Bailey Babies (The Baileys #6.5)

BUZZ WHEEL PRESS RELEASE: Don't drink the Lake Starlight water! Bailey babies are busy growing in their mommies' tummies and the Baileys are having a triple baby shower to celebrate. If you want in on the pool on who pops first and when, contact me.

Operation Bailey Birthday (The Baileys #9.5)

BUZZ WHEEL PRESS RELEASE: Rumor around town is a certain matriarch of the Bailey family is having a BIG BIRTHDAY! It's even spurred a few of the Bailey kids to return home to celebrate with their beloved great-grandmother, Dori. In fact, now that there are twenty-six Bailey great-grandchildren the event is going to be overflowing with laughter and love. Also... I heard that Piper & Rayne have been speaking to some of the kids (i.e. Calista, Maverick, Easton, Brinley and Palmer) and so we're getting some special POV's. I can't wait to report my findings the day after the party!

OPERATION
bailey wedding

A NOVELLA

PIPER RAYNE

LAKE STARLIGHT BUZZ WHEEL

BUZZ WHEEL PRESS RELEASE: No one could have guessed a marriage could sprout from a one-night stand, but Holly Radcliffe and Austin Bailey appear to be written in the stars. From the backseat of Austin's Jeep to the altar they go. Our entire town has been prepping for the event of the year, but as usual things never go smoothly. If you have the inside scoop on any of it be sure to let me know!

1

———

Holly

Five days until the wedding...

"Get back, doggies." I nudge Myles and Daisy with my legs as I slide into the house with my wedding dress in my arms.

"Hol?" Austin yells from the kitchen.

"You stay right there!" I yell back.

"Why?" His voice is growing closer, so I kick off my flip-flops and head for the stairs.

"I have my dress. You can't see it."

"You don't actually believe in that superstition, do you? I want to see you alone on our wedding day before, not in front of everyone. I want a moment..."

His voice drowns out when I slam the guest bedroom door. I hang up my dress, ignoring the four paws scratching outside the door. They act like the room is overfilled with chew toys, treats, and a smorgasbord of steak.

"Relax, Myles and Daisy. Go see Austin."

Myles whimpers under the door but Daisy's four paws prance on the hardwood floors we just installed throughout the whole house. Our first major change in our quest to transform it from Austin's family's home into our own. I still hold my breath every time one of his siblings comes over for a visit. They tell me it's okay, but I understand what it's like to be blindsided. I thought I had all my daddy issues worked out before running into him after my final dress fitting this evening.

He asked me questions about the wedding and wondered if his invitation got lost in the mail. Needless to say, there's no love lost between the two of us.

I unzip the garment bag, letting the dress hang out to make sure the puffy layers don't wrinkle before the big day. As I stand back and admire its beauty, I want to pinch myself that the day I'll become Mrs. Holly Bailey is right around the corner. I'll keep my maiden name for work purposes only because it's tricky when the principal and the science teacher have the same last name. A name that is very well known in Lake Starlight.

I'm not fooling anyone, half the town will be attending our wedding in the town square. If they weren't invited, they'll still have a chance to stand witness.

"Babe!" Austin yells from downstairs, probably ready to talk about more of his wants when it comes to the wedding. I've never heard of a man who pays attention to the details. Isn't he supposed to just be happy and show up?

"I'm coming." I slide out of the room with one more glance at my dress. "Let's go, Myles." I pat his head and head down the stairs. I'm not sure where Daisy got off to.

Myles walks down with me, stair for stair. Austin's waiting at the bottom of the stairs.

He has a glass of wine in hand because I called him on the way home, so he knows I ran into my father tonight. It's not like we haven't talked about the possibility of my father attending our nuptials, we have. At length. Austin thinks I'll regret not having him as a guest whereas I say he's never been a real father to me, so why would I care? But I don't get angry when he brings it up because he's coming from the place of a son that doesn't have the option of having either of his parents there.

"Thanks," I mumble, taking the glass from his hand and sipping its sweet goodness. "Perfect."

"The sun is setting behind the trees and it's beautiful. Come." He puts his arm around my shoulders and leads me into the kitchen and through the sliding glass doors onto the outside deck overlooking the property.

Austin's a consistent strong body for me to lean on when it comes to my issues with my dad. But what my dad has done to his family complicates things.

We sit down in a set of deck chairs and I prop my feet up on the small table in front of us. Austin was right. The sky is lit up with pink, yellow, and orange colors as far as the eye can see. It's breathtaking. The glowing sun slides down the horizon giving us our first glimpse of the sky full of stars that will take over.

The best decision I ever made was taking that temporary principal position to find my father. It led me to Austin, so I guess in some small way, my father brought me the best man who's ever entered my life.

"So?" he says.

"What?"

He raises his eyebrows staring at me until I fess up.

"He asked if his invite got lost. I mean the nerve of him." I sip my wine.

"That's not really a surprise." My fiancé settles in next to me, putting his arm around me. "You gotta ask yourself, babe, do you really not want him there?"

"I have no idea. I mean my mom will be there... Savannah..."

The last thing I want is the police called to my wedding.

"Don't worry about them. This is about you. Do *you* want him there?"

I traveled thousands of miles for the man, only to find out he has a brand new family he dotes on after leaving my life completely when I was young. A part of me is not even sure he'd want to come, and the possible rejection makes me gun-shy.

"Come here." Austin pats his lap and I crawl into his big body. "I love you," he whispers in my ear. "All I care about is that you walk down that aisle to me. The rest is just noise. If you want him there, I'll handle Savannah and your mom too if you want. If you don't, then cool, no biggie."

I grip my arms around his neck a little tighter. "How did I ever get so lucky?"

He chuckles into my neck, his thumb running along the bare skin between my shirt and my shorts. "I'm the lucky one. I can't believe I almost gave you up."

"I can't believe I almost let you go." I draw back from our embrace and press my hand on his cheek. "Just noise, right?"

He smiles, that light-up-my-heart one that says all we need in this world is us. "Noise. Now let me distract you." His tongue slides up my neck until his teeth latch on to my earlobe. "Let's make some noise of our own."

I giggle and feel his hardness under my ass. "That was cheesy."

His hands run up my back, pulling me closer. "You telling me my lines are shit?" His mouth casts open kisses along my neck, and he arches me to expose my chest. Just when the fabric of my shirt stops him, his hand slides along my waist to flick a button on my shirt open.

"I love your lines."

"There's the right answer." Another button releases, then another.

"Out here though?" I look behind us, wondering when a Bailey sibling may surprise us.

"After you said my lines suck? I have to prove myself."

He pats my ass to get up and I rise to my feet, missing him immediately. But before I can fully miss him, his fingers flick the button of my shorts and he lowers the zipper. "My favorite color," he says, sliding them down my legs and leaning forward to press a kiss right between my legs.

"Austin," I sigh.

His hands move up and he undoes my shirt one button at a time, blindly moving it off my shoulders as his lips kiss all over my stomach. "Can't wait until you have my baby in here."

My heart grows wings with his words. Austin isn't shy about wanting us to start a family right away. I'm sure part of it is due to losing his parents at such a young age. When Calista, his niece, made a surprise appearance, it only spurred him further to want a little Bailey of his own. Once Dion was born, even more so.

"Let's practice," he stares up at me with hope in his eyes. This has been another merry-go-round conversation the past few months.

"Okay," I agree, just wanting to be close to him. Besides, it's less than a week until we're married.

I went off the pill six months ago due to my age and the chance for blood clots, but we've been using condoms, much to Austin's dislike. But I refused to be standing at the altar with a burgeoning belly under my wedding gown.

"Really?" The smile that transforms his face is nothing short of magical.

I'd have ten of his babies if I got that look every time.

"Really," I say and lean in for a quick kiss.

He leans back, pulls his track shorts down. "Well then?"

"Austin!"

He laughs, pulling me so that I'm straddling him, and his hard length is pressed to my center. "I'm kidding. Come here."

Our lips meet, his tongue sliding into my mouth. I could kiss this man every minute of every day for the rest of my life.

His fingers graze down my ribs and slide into my panties, pushing them to the side so he can enter me. The ache between my legs grows with each second that passes.

"Jeez, seriously, you two. Aren't you supposed to be over this by now and be like an old married couple?"

"Phoenix!" Austin yells, positioning me away from her, but there's no hiding anything.

"I'm home." Her laugh trails off inside the house when she leaves the sliding glass door. "Myles, get off Daisy. You're as bad as your owners."

Austin hovers over me. "One week and they're all going away, right?"

I smile up at him. "Please, we both know that's not the truth."

His head falls to my chest and he sucks one of my nipples into his mouth through my bra.

"Let's go see why she's here three days early." I wiggle under him and he climbs off me, pulling up his pants and picking up my shirt and shorts.

"Sometimes I hate my big family," he says.

"Aw... you know that's a lie. And don't worry, we can have wild sex later."

We walk into the house to find five suitcases by the stairway. Turning to one another, we share a look of bewilderment.

"Or not?" I raise an eyebrow.

Phoenix is sitting on the couch, her head buried in her phone.

"Phoenix?" I ask.

"So, LA isn't panning out."

Austin's head falls back, and he sighs.

Looks like we have a new roommate for a while.

2

____

Wyatt

"Denver, what are you doing? Move to the right! You're gonna hit the wall," Kingston yells at his brother while they try to move my dresser up the stairs of Brooklyn's and my new house.

"Denver, we just painted. Your sister will have a conniption." I follow behind them with a garment box in my hands.

"Couldn't you have hired movers? Aren't you like a millionaire or something? Why am I waking up at the ass crack of dawn to move you into your huge farmhouse."

"It's not a farmhouse. They don't have those in Alaska," Kingston says.

Denver lowers the dresser just to give him _the_ annoyed look.

"What?"

"Did you see the long front porch that faces the mountains?" Denver asks.

"Nothing else about it says farmhouse and they don't have a farm so..."

"Can we please just move," I say because I'm not going to stand here on the stairs while they argue.

"Let's go, weakling," Kingston says, walking up the stairs.

"Weakling?" Denver guffaws.

"I'm the one facing backward."

I ignore the brother-bickering until they get the dresser into our master bedroom. When they go downstairs to get more of our stuff, I look around the room. At the bed we bought to start over. My dresser and nightstands. A few paintings Brooklyn loves. Veering out of the room, I pass the three other empty bedrooms and wonder when we'll fill them.

In order to do that, I need to ask Brooklyn to marry me, but with Austin and Holly's wedding in five days and us deciding to move into this house the same week, it's been too hectic. So, I've decided not to pop the question until next week.

"Brook is here!" Kingston yells. "Holy shit. What does she have with her?"

I shake my head because if she bought one more thing for this house, we're going to be house poor. The woman is constantly shopping for knickknacks and other useless decorative items.

Nevertheless, I'm eager to see her since we parted earlier, and she kept her destination a secret. My feet hit the bottom step and I see her holding a small box with holes.

Gizmo is at her heels, barking and jumping.

"Stop it Giz." She shoos him away with her leg.

"What do you have there?" Denver asks.

Brooklyn looks up at the house, seeing me in the doorway. She has the same look on her face as she did when she bought the new kitchen table I told her we didn't need.

She walks up the steps and places the box on the porch. Gizmo circles it, continuing to bark. Brooklyn picks him up in her arms. "Shh... you'll scare them."

Her eyes find mine because now I know it's a living being.

"We said no cats, Brook." I lean my shoulder against the doorframe.

"It's not a cat."

Denver peeks inside the lid and falls to his ass in laughter. "You're kidding me, right?"

"We need something to do with all this space. And if we get more, we can have fresh eggs every day." She looks around to the nothingness around us. One of the biggest reasons we purchased this place.

My shoulders sag. "We don't need to raise chickens. Gizmo is going to hate them." Just as I make my argument, Gizmo jumps out of Brooklyn's arms, lunging for the box, but Kingston grabs hold of him.

"That's not food," he tells him.

I stare at Brooklyn. She's smiling and happy.

What can I say? I'm a sucker.

"How many are there?"

She bites her lips.

"Brook?"

"Five."

"Five?" My voice is calm even though inside, I can already see how this is going to turn out. Me figuring out how to keep chickens alive in the wilds of Alaska. Where are they going to go in the winter?

"See it's a farmhouse," Denver says, heading back to the

truck because he must know that his sister and I need to have a conversation.

She walks toward me, already leaving the chicks abandoned. Luckily, Kingston dropped Gizmo into the small fenced area I made for him on one end of the porch.

"Why chickens?" I ask.

"Why not?" She runs her finger down my sweaty t-shirt.

"I could name about one hundred reasons why not."

"But?" Her eyes are wide and hopeful as she holds my gaze.

I shake my head. "If we're in this together, you better start consulting me."

"What would you have said?" She steps closer so that we're almost chest-to-chest. Her blonde hair is pulled into a messy bun and all I want to do is unleash those wild strands and tug her toward me.

"We would've talked about it."

"And?"

"I would've said to wait until after we're settled."

She tilts her head and bites her lip. My complete undoing and she knows it. "But they needed homes and it's like we're starting this next chapter of our life together with them."

"Come here." I loop my finger into the waist of her shorts and pull her toward me.

"Are you sweaty?" she asks.

"Yes, because I'm here moving us in while you're out buying chickens." I lean forward and press my lips to hers.

"I got one for you."

"I think you got five for me."

She loops her arms around my neck, her fingers playing with the back of my hair. "But one is especially for you."

My hands splay on her ass, pushing her toward me. "Tell me you didn't buy a cock?"

She laughs and swats at my chest. "There's only one cock in this house."

I nod, still not convinced.

"Yours, I named Manhattan. She's dark and mysterious and reminds me of you. A little standoffish to the others."

"And where are we going to keep these little ladies?"

"We're going to build a chicken coop."

I shake my head. "*You're* going to build a chicken coop." I kiss her and guide her to the side with my hand on her hip.

"I thought we're a team?"

I stare down at the box. "We are, but this wasn't a team decision."

"Wyatt!" she calls out as I make my way back over to the moving truck.

When I get to the back of the vehicle, I find Kingston and Denver sitting on our sofa, two beers in hand.

"It's ten in the morning," I say.

They look at one another and shrug.

Damn bachelors.

"Chickens, huh?" Denver says, standing from the couch.

"Get used to it, man, she's got a soft heart. I mean look, she took you in." Kingston pats my back, jumping down from the truck.

Denver pushes the couch toward the end of the truck, and I grab the one side, Kingston the other.

"I just put her in charge of building the coop, so neither of you help her."

"Don't you have a heart, man?" Kingston asks.

I furrow my forehead in question.

"The coop is going to fall and kill the chickens if Brooklyn builds it."

I shake my head, passing her as she tries to get the kit she bought out of my truck. She blows at a strand of blonde hair that's snuck out of her ponytail holder. She's adorable already. I'm going to enjoy watching her struggle building that thing. At least for a while. We both know that in the end, I'll help her.

Strike that, I'll be doing it all myself.

3

Rome

Four days until the wedding...

The food delivery truck pulls up out back of Terra and Mare and they pull out the ramp on the back. Colin steps up to help our delivery guy get all the food I need for the rehearsal dinner into the restaurant.

I hear her before I see her. "Check out this pretty girl." Harley walks in with Calista trailing behind. She's wearing her flower girl dress and has a huge smile on her face. Dion is strapped to Harley's chest in one of those fabric wraps. I'm still not sure I trust that thing.

Calista twirls in a circle to showcase her puffy white dress.

"You look beautiful." I bend down to hold my hand out for her. We do a short dance until I pick her up and circle her around. "Will you save the first dance for me?"

"Nope." She presses her lips together.

With age two came an attitude and now that she's a few months off three, it's even worse. I'm trying to adjust to this new personality. Harley says she's testing limits and she'd be right.

"Who gets the first dance then?" I ask.

"I wanna dance with Holly."

I nod, looking over to Harley. She shrugs, a smile teasing her lips while her hands run down Dion's small body.

"I get it. The bride."

"Yep." She nods enthusiastically.

"We went to Holly's final dress fitting yesterday... someone has the wedding bug," Harley fills me in on where this obsession was created.

"And that's why you're wearing your flower girl dress?"

A loud bang from the truck shocks her and she jolts in my arms.

"We're only wearing it on a short walk and then taking it off because we don't want to get it dirty." Harley eyes Calista which means there was a long talk and heavy negotiations on that decision.

"You know Mommy's going to be a bride," Calista says.

Harley shakes her head at me. We discuss this daily. She's not ready to leave Dion and he's not ready to fly. We want to elope with just the four of us. We'll give it a few months and then I'll make the reservations. She wants a beach wedding and what Harley wants, Harley gets.

"Let's go get you a dress," I say to her.

Harley laughs and shakes her head. "I don't need a dress." She steps up and puts her arm on our daughter's back.

I bend down and kiss Dion's small head sprinkled with light brown hair.

"You'd be pretty."

"Mommy's pretty no matter what she's wearing," Calista says.

"Even if it's nothing," I say and grin.

Harley smacks me, probably because she knows our daughter is in a copycat stage.

"Come on, Calista. Let's let Daddy work."

I put Calista down on the ground and she takes Harley's hand. "I just have to get this order in and then I'll be up." I kiss her on the lips.

"I'm going to try to lay down after our walk if I can get them both down for a nap."

I let my lips linger over hers. "Is that an invitation?"

"It hasn't been six weeks yet."

"I can't work with these limitations. It kind of makes me not want to get you pregnant again."

She laughs and her lips brush along mine. "That's not to say there aren't other things I can do." She lets her hand trail down my chest.

I glance over and find Calista playing twenty questions with Colin about what's in the boxes, so I reach out and slyly grab her ass.

"Nah, it's not much fun if I can't get you off." I squeeze her ass cheek.

"Spoken like a true Prince Charming."

With one more peck, we disengage and as always when she's not at my side, I miss her.

"Come on, Calista. Let's go." She waves her over and Calista skips to me, hugs me and then takes Harley's hand.

I walk them both out through the kitchen and dining area to the front door of the restaurant.

We say our goodbyes and I watch my entire life walk down Main Street for a walk, wishing I could join them. A warm sensation warms in my heart. My love for them is so strong and so pure it's almost scary sometimes.

With a smile, I turn to make my way back into the kitchen.

"What time do you start serving?" Liam's hand lands on my shoulder and his gravelly voice sounds in my ear.

"I'm just shut down between lunch and dinner. What's up?" I study my best friend for a second. He looks like shit.

"Your sister is driving me crazy. Did you know she has a specific way she likes the dishes placed in the dishwasher? As if it makes a difference."

I laugh. "All right, for you, I'm open."

I poke my head into the back and check with Colin that he has it handled. I really need to give him a raise, so he never leaves me.

Walking over to the bar area, I join Liam where he sits on one of the bar stools. "Hard stuff or beer?"

"Beer. I have a client coming to the shop in an hour."

I nod. "So it's been rough, has it? You know my sister... she's anal and compulsive and sometimes bitchy."

He takes a long pull of his beer after I pass it to him. "Her and Denver are complete opposites. I'm constantly picking up after him and she still finds a way to criticize my way of organizing shit."

"I have no idea why you agreed to either of them living with you in the first place." I rest my back along the bar and cross my arms.

Liam's been my best friend since grade school. There are few things I don't know about him. But I do know that I've never quite understood him and Savannah. When we were young, I took it as the older sister crush thing. Sav is four years older than us, so at thirteen, she was seventeen and a senior in high school. No one has to figure out why I'd catch him looking at her.

As we've gotten older, I've tried to ignore the lingering gazes. How he can always tell me where to find her in a crowded room and sometimes who she's talking to. He tracks her movements and watches her. Yet he still razzes her for a reaction like we used to do at twelve. I thought it was a horrible idea that she move in with him—even temporarily. No way do I want to lose my best friend because he wants to nail my sister.

"I didn't have a choice. Your grandma said it was a good idea and everyone knows you can't, and shouldn't, tell grandma Dori she's wrong." He takes another pull on his beer, his eyes everywhere but on me.

"How much longer until her place is all fixed?"

"Insurance is still dicking her around."

"As long as that's the only thing dicking her." I level my gaze on him and he tries to give me a look of complete disgust, like 'as if' but then his gaze drops to the bar top and I can tell it's an act.

I cringe. They're either going to kill each other or fuck each other before this is over and either way, I lose my best friend.

I hope like hell Denver can intervene before either happens. If only I could get one of them to date someone else. It sucks to think about needing them apart, but Savannah and Liam could never be a forever thing. They're too different, too opposite. Savannah appreciates sophistication and Liam likes his girls... Well, I guess I don't really know his type at all. He usually just likes them willing and able and beyond that, I haven't seen consistency on his part. Which means he's great as a friend, not so much as a potential suitor for my sister.

"Then I guess you should live and breathe the business until she leaves. I'd take her in if I could."

He finishes his beer. "It makes the most sense that she's at my place...I have so much extra room. It's just... hard to live with her."

I don't ask what's so hard. Is it only her nit-picky nature or did he catch her coming out of the shower? Ew... I can't believe that thought just crossed my mind. But if my inkling is true, it has to be hell on him being in such close proximity every day.

"I better get going." He stands from the bar stool.

I watch him for a minute. The long face and deep-set eyes from lack of sleep.

"Anything else you want to talk about?" I ask before he has a chance to leave.

He stops at the door, turns my way. I know my best friend and the look on his face is tortured, even if he's trying not to show it. Savannah's the one thing he can't be straight up honest with me about.

"Nah. Thanks for the beer." He pushes the door open and leaves Terra and Mare no different than when he showed up.

He'll talk when he's ready to admit it to himself. Liam doesn't give one shit what anyone thinks. He goes after what he wants without apology. I can't imagine Savannah would be any different. But if he thinks he's going to touch one hair on my sister's head before talking to me first, he's got another think coming.

4

____

Austin

"Damn it," I murmur, watching one of my players slide into home on a steal putting us up by a run.

"I didn't figure that'd be your response when we took the lead." Jack pats me on the back.

"If we win, we go to state."

"Um... yeah, that's a good thing."

"Not when your honeymoon is at the same time."

When we planned the honeymoon, Lake Starlight had no shot at state, but something turned around a quarter into the season and the team found a groove that led us into the regional finals.

I glance back at Holly. She smiles and claps, but her eyes dictate another feeling. One of dread that I'll be on a beach with her while Jack manages my team through the state tournament.

I hate that I'm conflicted. I shouldn't be. We didn't even

make state the year I had Elijah. Who's also in the stands with Becca by his side. How those two have beaten the odds the last few years, I'm still unsure of, but JP is on the other side of Elijah talking shit about the last play.

"I've got you handled." Jack pats me on the back again.

I nod. Jack's a great coach. He'll do fantastic. I could probably ask Elijah and JP to help out if needed, but it's me not being there that cuts deep. The guilt sucks because I love Holly and I *want* to be on a beach with her. Take her inside one of those cabanas until we're breathless and sweaty. I want to swim in the ocean late at night and have days where we never leave the bed.

The other team scores a run in the bottom and the game goes into overtime. Each team is given a five-minute break for water.

"Hey, handsome." Holly comes to the fence line.

I circle around the gate and she hugs me around the stomach. "You're supposed to smile when your team makes a comeback."

I plaster on a smile, but we both know it doesn't reach my eyes.

She sighs. "We can stay back." She repeats the conversation we've had numerous times.

"No. We're not doing that. I trust Jack. He's a good coach and he can handle it." I'm sure I sound like I'm trying to convince myself.

"The option is there if you want it."

"I don't."

"Okay but—"

I press my lips to hers and when I draw back, I rest my forehead against hers. "I don't."

She nods. "Then go out there and kick some ass."

"HOLLY!" Grandma Dori stands up from where she's sitting on the bleachers.

We both turn to her. "Can you get me a pretzel? No salt though. My blood pressure."

Holly nods and turns back to me.

"Sorry."

She shrugs. "For what? Don't ever be sorry. I love your family and I love you… whether we're here or we're in Hawaii."

"We're going to be in Hawaii."

She smiles and nods. "Okay. I'll get my bikini ready to pack."

"No need for any clothes."

She giggles and I take the opportunity to give her another kiss. God, I love her. She's giving me the out I feel I need.

"Go get 'em, Coach." Her hand trails down my stomach. "I have to go buy a pretzel. With no salt." She turns on her heels and heads for the concession.

I watch her go and then head back in the dugout, talking with Jack about our next move. He offers some good suggestions, proving his coaching skills. I trust him. I do.

We end up winning the game eight to six and my heart shouldn't sink as my players are running off the field, huddling together and screaming. Our team shakes hands with the competition, and I think I might squeeze a few hands harder than necessary.

After the game is over, Holly's at the fence line with Grandma Dori and Phoenix, talking with Elijah, JP, and Becca.

Jack kisses Grandma Dori and Holly on the cheek when we reach them.

"Way to go, Austin," Grandma says, patting my cheek.

"Thanks."

"I gotta go. We're playing Liars Poker at the home tonight."

"What's that?" Holly tries to look interested, but my grandmother and her weekly game nights with her friends isn't what's on my mind or hers right now.

"Come and find out," Grandma Dori says.

Holly looks over to me.

"Wedding stuff," I say, giving her the out.

"Oh, that reminds me." Grandma Dori's eyes widen. "I dropped off the pictures you were asking for this afternoon. Neither one of you were home, so I let myself in."

I groan. Holly shoots me a look to say 'be nice' it was good of her to do that. The fact that she still has a key sucks, but it feels too awkward to ask for it back and worse if I changed the locks on her, so we suffer through her impromptu drop-ins.

"Thanks. Did you put them in the room?" Holly asks.

"The wedding room?" I add, making fun of Holly because that room is off limits to me.

She ignores me.

"Yep, left them there with the rest of your things."

"Thank you so much. I have the picture frames to put them in. I can't wait for you to see what I arranged for our loved ones who couldn't be with us."

Grandma Dori smiles sweetly. She loves Holly. "I saw the dress. It's gorgeous."

Holly's face lights up. "Don't you love it?"

"It turned out wonderful."

"I wouldn't know because I'm only allowed to see it at the altar," I grumble.

"Austin wants to see me before I walk down the aisle," Holly says to Grandma Dori and if you went off looks alone, you'd think I just said I wanted her to walk down the aisle to "You Shook Me All Night Long" by AC/DC.

"That's not customary or traditional and it's bad luck. Now rain. If there's rain, you know that's good luck. It was a torrential downpour when I married your grandfather. My wedding dress was ruined but look how long we lasted."

I pull Holly to my side.

"That's what I said," Holly says, looking up at me with an 'I told you so' in her expression.

"I want a moment between just us," I say.

"You'll get that after the ceremony. Don't make me keep bodyguards on you." My grandma waggles her finger in front of my face like I'm five.

Pretty sure I can give my brothers a bottle of Jack and sneak out before they'd ever know.

"Don't you have to go play Liars Poker?" I ask.

She rolls her eyes like it's a nuisance, but she loves her games, especially when she wins. "Yes, but this time I'm telling Ethel to shut down her hearing aid. We'll be in the middle of a hand and she answers her phone on the damn thing."

"On her hearing aid?" I ask.

"Yeah, I need to upgrade soon." She taps her ear.

"So you can answer your phone calls during a conversation?" Holly asks.

"I can't have Ethel out-do me." She waves me off and kisses my cheek. "Love you."

Doing the same to Holly, she's out and heading toward her car in the parking lot.

"Why is she still driving when the Sheriff told her to stop?" I ask Holly.

She laughs. "Because she's Dori. I'm not sure she'll ever stop doing what she wants."

I swing my arm over her shoulders. "Come on."

We head out of the stadium to my Jeep and the ride home is quiet. Too quiet. I'm thinking about missing my team going to state for the first time since I took over and Holly's probably thinking about how I'm thinking about it. I know she'd understand but what kind of message would it send if I asked her to postpone our honeymoon?

When we arrive home, I turn on the grill and she heads upstairs, probably to do wedding stuff.

A blood-curdling scream a few minutes later has me racing up the stairs, jumping over Daisy as she tries to catch Myles.

"Babe!"

"Don't come in."

She's in the wedding room and I can tell she's crying from the hitch in her voice.

"Why, are you crying?" I ask.

She sounds like an injured animal. "Just... it's my wedding dress. Grandma Dori must've left the door open and one of the dogs peed all over the bottom of my dress."

My forehead hits the door with a thud. *Shit.*

5
____

Brooklyn

Three Days before the wedding

"This is bullshit," I mumble, throwing the screwdriver thingy to the side. I stare at the chicken coop and it's lopsided and looking nothing like the directions say it should. Kingston is right, I'm going to kill my chicks before they can ever lay an egg.

"You okay?" Wyatt comes out of the house and hands me a glass of lemonade.

He's really thriving with this homemaker shit. Even starting a garden in the back corner for vegetables. I'm over here failing at my first project.

"I'm fine. Just go over there to your tomato plants."

He sits down next to me, his knees propped up with a glass of lemonade hanging from his hands between his legs.

"Want some help?" he asks.

I glance to him at my side. "No."

"Okay." He shifts to get up.

"Ugh... sit."

"Excuse me?"

"Please just sit down."

He does.

He hasn't made me feel guilty about the chickens, but he hasn't helped me with any of the work either. I think he's trying to teach me a lesson, but then again, our new kitchen table arrived yesterday, and he didn't mind christening it last night. I'm getting a lot of mixed signals from him.

"So you do want help?" he asks.

I sigh.

He waits patiently because he's so much more patient than I am. He'd probably have this chicken coop already built, but after step one I was already annoyed.

"I'm sorry, okay?"

He chuckles, turns my way with that lottery winning smile. "You're sorry?"

I throw my hands in the air. "I'm sorry for buying the chickens without talking to you first."

"We're a team."

"I know, but you brought Gizmo home without consulting me."

The dog hears his name and prances over, lying between us with his belly up in the air. I pet him and his two front paws cover my hand in a plea for me to continue.

"That's different. You wanted a dog. I don't remember saying I wanted chickens."

I roll my eyes, but he does have a point. "Why do you always have to be right?"

He picks up Gizmo and puts him on the other side of

him. The dog whines but Wyatt ignores him and puts his arm behind me and one hand on my cheek.

"It's not about being right. I just want the consideration. You know I'll give you whatever you want and that includes chickens. I'm going to help you with this chicken coop, but this is gonna be a lot of work."

I place my hand over his. He's right and I hate that he's right. All the damn time. "I'm sorry."

"There's my girl." He leans forward, his lips pressing to mine, and a moan slips up my throat.

He lays me back in the grass and then he's on top of me, parting my legs with his thighs to make room for himself.

"You're beautiful when you're frustrated." He circles his lips and I can feel his bulge through his track pants. "Watching you all afternoon with the power tools, bending over with that ass I love up in the air? It's been hard not to come over sooner."

"Why didn't you?"

He chuckles, his fingers brushing my hair off my face. "I like to torture myself."

"And me apparently."

He kisses my forehead. "Never you. I don't like torturing you." He kisses my nose. "But I kind of like that this is our backyard and there aren't neighbors in sight. I love that I can strip you bare right here and push inside you with one thrust and no one would be the wiser."

"What's up with all the talk? Why don't you just do it?" I wiggle under him, positioning him right where I want him.

"Why Miss Bailey, are you asking me to fuck you in broad daylight with no one but Gizmo watching?"

"And the chicks," I add. Locking my arms around him, I pull his lips to mine, but he hovers over them for a second. "Fuck me, Mr. Whitmore."

That does it.

My clothes are torn off and flung somewhere in the grass while we frantically move our lips and hands all over one another. Under the blue sky with huge white clouds, Wyatt and I christen our backyard.

"THE HOUSE LOOKS GREAT, BROOK." Savannah sits on the edge of my bed. "It reminds me of our house growing up. You even have the lake." She looks out the back window. Our lake is closer than my parents', but she's right, the lake was a big selling feature for me.

"I wouldn't have this without Wyatt." I continue to put away some clothes we've yet to unpack.

Savannah's gaze is everywhere except on the box of picture frames she's unpacking. "You bought it together."

I shrug. She's right, but this is all thanks to Wyatt's money. My essential oil company is making a profit, but the hotel is in the black and thriving since Wyatt bought it. It's his money no matter how much he says it's ours.

"If we break up, I move out. I hate that. I wanted to put down half, but I couldn't afford it."

Savannah sighs. "You're partners. What's his is yours and what's yours is yours." We both laugh. "Seriously though, you're too hung up on the money issue."

"And what about you? What are you hung up on?" I sit on the bed next to her.

Savannah's life is in a huge upheaval. She's been kicked out of her home because of a flood and is living with two men who party like wild animals. "Are they bringing home girls?"

She unwraps another picture frame and sets it aside. It's

a photo of just the Bailey girls. "Denver has occasionally, but not as much as I would've thought."

"And Liam?"

She shakes her head. Just like I thought, he's the problem.

"I've always liked Liam. He seems a little more respectable than our brothers."

"Maybe that's because he's not our brother," she says.

"Yeah, but he's always felt like he was."

She stares at me like I just escaped an insane asylum. Because while I might view Liam like a brother and Juno might and Phoenix and Sedona might, I don't think Sav has ever viewed him that way.

"How are you guys getting along? I'm surprised you haven't killed one another yet." I knock her with my shoulder.

She laughs and her finger runs along the edge of the picture frame. "I'm annoying him. He didn't even come home last night."

I place my hand on her knee. "Do you want to talk about anything?

Seeing her so down is hard. Savannah was our pseudo mom after our parents died. With her being only two years older than me, it's weird that she's always felt so much older because she took on so much so young.

"Just about how you got Wyatt out there building a chicken coop." She smiles. It's fake but there. I should've known she'd hide whatever it is that's bothering her. That's Savannah, but sometimes I think she trusts Austin more than the rest of us because they both pushed their dreams aside so all of us could pursue ours. Austin got Holly, but Savannah's still taking one for the team.

I squeeze her knee and stand, going back to unpack

Wyatt's stuff. The least I can do is put away his clothes now that he's taken over chicken coop construction.

"I probably would've killed them. I'm not handy with wood and nails it turns out."

Savannah works a little faster to unwrap a few more picture frames. Her melancholy mood is shifting. Either that or she's trying to force whatever is bothering her to the back of her mind.

"He's doing a great job. It looks cute." She's staring out the window again and I glance over at her, but something else has caught my eye. In the bottom of the box, shoved between two pairs of jeans is a small ring-sized box.

"Savannah?" I say my voice low like I'm looking at a bomb that could go off any second.

Savannah doesn't turn from the window, her eyes glued to whatever she sees.

"What were you saying?" she asks like she wasn't just lost for a moment.

"There's a small box in here."

"Okay, open it," she says.

I shake my head. "I can't. I think it's a ..."

Realization dawns on her face and she smiles because we all knew it was a matter of time, but I had no idea that he'd already bought the ring.

Just then we hear the backdoor open. "Brook!" Wyatt yells.

Savannah rushes over, helping me put all his clothes back in the box while two sets of footsteps barrel up the steps.

Doing a crisscross thing with the lid, I close the box at the last second and kick it to the side just as Wyatt steps into the room. He glances around but smiles at us.

"Hey Savannah," he says, then looks at me. "I asked

Liam to come over and help. I can't figure this one part out. How about we order some dinner or something?" My naive Wyatt stands with nothing but optimism on his face with Liam standing a few steps behind him.

"Shit, you know I just remembered I had an appointment rebook from earlier this week, and I have to get to the shop," Liam says, gripping the back of his neck with his hand.

"I'm going to take Grandma Dori to get her new hearing aid. I'll come back tomorrow and help Brooklyn." Savannah slides past him. "Great house, Wyatt."

They both leave and Wyatt and I watch out the front window as they get into separate cars, pulling away without a word to one another.

"Do you think we should ask Savannah if she wants to move in here?" I lean my back to Wyatt's chest.

"Believe it or not, babe, I think she's exactly where she should be." He wraps his arms around my waist, and I stare at my hands over his. My left hand is bare, and I can't help but wonder when he's planning on proposing.

Damn it! This is all I'm going to think about now.

6

Denver

I walk into the tuxedo place and Austin is already there wearing his, standing on the pedestal with a man's hands running up his legs.

"I thought this was just the pick-up?" I ask, sitting down in a chair, pulling out my cookie from the Lard Have Mercy bag in my hand.

"It is, but my pants were about five inches too short so now they're going to rush this. Nothing is going as planned." Having a brother who had to take the reins of a family when I was younger means it's not a mystery when he's stressed.

"I heard about the dress." I take a bite of the cookie and take a moment to admire its chewy goodness.

Austin stares at me quizzingly in the reflection of the mirror.

I hold up the bag of the diner his soon-to-be mother-in-law works at.

He nods in understanding. "The dry cleaner thinks they can get it out, but damn she was a mess."

"And then your team made state?"

He nods in the mirror, widening his legs farther. "Yeah, that sucks, too. Plus, I have the whole issue of her dad."

I finish my cookie and crumple the bag into a ball. "What do you need me to do? Put Savannah in a restraining jacket during the ceremony?"

He chuckles. Thank God, I've always tried to be his comic relief ever since our parents died.

"Denver," another man who works there calls out. He has a tuxedo in his hand, so I suppose I'm supposed to try it on.

I stand but turn around when I hear the bell above the door ring. In walks Rome. "Rome!" I boom.

"Jack's right behind me and Kingston texted me to say he's running five minutes late." He sits down in the chair I just vacated. "Looking good, big bro." He puts his ankle on his opposite knee.

Sometimes I'm envious of my brother. He's my twin and left me behind to live his life with Harley. The whole thing happened so fast I worried I'd never find my place in this new life of his. But Harley's great. And the fact that I have a niece and a nephew to spoil, and thereby piss off their parents, is a great bonus.

But we're so much alike I wonder what made him switch gears so fast and whether I should consider doing the same. Even Liam keeps denying my invites to go out and drink. I've brought only a couple of girls home since Savannah's been there and you'd think I erased Excel from her computer. It didn't help that when I woke up the next day, one of them was in her panties and cami making breakfast for Liam. Sav did *not* like that.

"We were just discussing a straitjacket for Savannah," I fill Rome in.

"This is about Holly's dad, right?"

"Yeah," Austin says with dread in his tone.

"I was there that night," Rome says. "I'm not sure a straitjacket would work. I mean, she had murder in her eyes."

I laugh, but I'm the only one. It makes me feel immature.

I head into the change room to try my tux on and step out a few minutes later. It fits like a glove. Perfect.

"Looks good," the man helping Austin says, eyeing me up and down. "You go and take it off," he tells Austin.

We exchange places while Jack walks in with his Hammer Time Hardware t-shirt on. He's been a good friend of Austin's through the years and is another guy who's now gotten married and is expecting his second kid or something. It's hard to keep up.

"You now." A woman points to Rome and sends him in. We're like a merry-go-round. Austin comes out later in his regular clothes and instantly starts talking to Jack about the state tournament and who they should start as pitcher.

"Perfect," the man says to me, not having to make one alteration.

"Did you hear that, boys? Perfect." I twirl around with a John Travolta move from *Saturday Night Fever*.

None of them seem impressed. Austin's rambling on and on about the baseball thing. I'm not sure why he doesn't tell Holly he can't go on their honeymoon. They're teachers. Well, he is and she's a principal, they have the entire summer to go to Hawaii. I don't get it.

On my way down the hall to get changed, the door chime rings again and in walks Wyatt, Kingston, and Liam. Thank God because they might've missed the funniest thing I've ever seen. I just spotted Rome coming out of the changing room with his tux on. Shit, my phone is back in the changing room.

"Aust, grab your phone, man." I nudge him.

Rome looks like a prisoner as he walks down the short hallway from the changing rooms to the three-way mirror.

"No need. I got this." Liam pulls out his phone.

"I'll be back-up," Kingston follows behind.

"Put that shit away. They mismeasured or some shit," Rome grumbles.

His pants are bulging at the waist and the button looks like it might pop off. The shirt is pulling with the buttons barely keeping it closed and giving us a glimpse of his non-flat stomach.

"No. No. You were the same as your brother." The woman looks through some paperwork in her hand.

"Step up," the man says and there's Rome looking like the tuxedo shrunk in a dryer.

"You look like the Hulk right before all his clothes pop off," Kingston says, sitting down on the coffee table, snapping pictures. "I'm so Snapchatting this shit."

Rome turns around and tries to grab the phone, but Kingston is faster and slides out of his way.

"You've got reflexes like Grandma Dori's side piece now." Kingston laughs.

"Grandma Dori doesn't have a side piece," I say.

"She's got that guy two doors down. I'm telling you, something is going on there."

I roll my eyes, Kingston sees jack shit.

"It's like that fat-man-in-a-tiny-suit skit Farley did on *Saturday Night Live*," Liam says.

I'm buckled over laughing and Rome's flipping us off in the mirror.

"My fiancée has been pregnant, I'm a chef who has to

taste his dishes and I can't fuck to expel any calories for six damn weeks. So piss off!" His face is all red and angry.

We all just laugh harder.

"Six weeks?" Wyatt asks. We all turn and look at him because of the surprise in his voice, which makes us all wonder. When our gaze turns his way, he rolls his eyes. "She's not pregnant."

We all sigh in unison.

"It goes by fast," Jack says.

"You don't understand, I like sex. A lot. So does Harley. Now I'm restricted to my hand like I'm back in high school." He holds it out and stares at it. "I'm getting calluses."

"Join Liam's club," I say.

"What's this?" Kingston asks, still snapping pictures of Rome.

"He's practically celibate. Doesn't ever go out since Sav moved in."

"That's not true," Liam plays it off.

The woman points to Kingston to tell him to go try his tux on. "Sorry, I gotta hear this. Jack?"

"He's busy," Austin says, probably still waiting to discuss baseball with him.

"I'll go." Wyatt volunteers because he's getting sex on the regular as disgusting as that thought is.

"Why don't you go out?" Kingston asks Liam.

I lean against the counter, snickering to myself.

"You start this shit on purpose." Liam points in my direction and I get the feeling that I should be on the look-out for saran wrap over the toilet or being woken up to the sound of clanking pots and pans at his place from now on.

I glance around the room. "All her brothers are here. Let's get this out in the open."

The light mood fades away. Rome stops the man from fussing with his tux and all eyes fall to Liam.

He swallows so deep, his Adam's apple bobs hard. "Shut the fuck up, Denver. I'm being polite. It's called being a gentleman."

I glance at Rome because we might not have that telepathic twin shit going on, but we do understand the dynamic between Liam and Savannah. We're too close not to know what's under all that hate.

"And what a gentleman you are! Except for when the two of you argue about clothes left in the dryer and how you stack the dishwasher."

"I get it. Savannah's not always easy," Austin says to Liam.

"It's fine. We're making do." He shoots me his evil stare and to think I finally gave him an out, but he didn't take it. I can't help but wonder what's really going on between them. Because I've never seen Liam so wound up before.

"Okay then. Let's go back and talk about Rome's new beer gut," Kingston says.

"It's not from beer, asshole." Rome's still pissed off. He's a second from breaking and it might just happen that Kingston's sporting a black eye at Austin's wedding.

7

Harley

Calista goes down for her nap and I'm rocking Dion when Rome opens the door to our apartment. I press my finger to my lips, and he slows his movements. Not that Dion can't sleep through a lot, we live above a restaurant in downtown Lake Starlight. It's not a metropolitan, but it's not as quiet as being on acres of land outside of town either.

"What's with the down face?" I whisper.

He leans forward and kisses me. "My tux didn't fit."

I purse my lips together. I've noticed Rome's new stomach a little, but he's been trying new dishes and when I was pregnant, I craved all the junk food, so it hasn't been easy for the man.

"We're not even married yet and I'm getting a gut."

"We're practically married. You have two kids, had to see me through one of the pregnancies. Plus you run a restaurant."

He silently swears to himself.

"I love you no matter your size," I say.

He rolls his eyes.

"Are you saying if I don't lose this baby weight, you're not going to love me?" I ask.

He opens the fridge, shuts it and flops down on the chair adjacent to me. "No, I love you and if your tits stay like that, I'll be a happy man." He winks.

"Post-pregnancy fact, they will not. As soon as I'm done breastfeeding they're going to look worse."

"Not to me."

With Dion's nose crinkled and his fists finally relaxing, I stand and place him in the bassinet.

"He's out?" Rome asks.

"Yeah." I come over to him and fall to my knees in front of him, placing my palms on his thighs and parting them. "I think you need a little attention." My fingers travel up to the button of his jeans. I flick them open and slide the zipper down.

"How can you even find me appealing? My dick is probably fat too."

I quirk an eyebrow. "Is that a bad thing?"

He chuckles, sliding down in the chair because we both know he needs my mouth on him. "I suppose not, but babe, I have a gut."

My hands slide up his stomach, raising his t-shirt and sure it's not perfectly flat with a six pack like before Dion, but it's not like he drinks a twelve pack every night.

"You're hot."

"I'm halfway to a dad bod."

I laugh, my head falling into his lap. "Then I love dad bods because I love your body."

His frown says he's still unconvinced, but I entice him to

raise his ass so I can slide his jeans off. I push them to his ankles and run my hand over his length, loving the feeling of it stiffening under my palm.

"You also did the tux fitting right after you and Li did the tasting for the fusion dishes you're working on. Do you know how much sodium you've had today?"

He hems and haws but grunts as I apply more pressure.

"Don't think about that right now. Just think about this." I run my thumb over the tip of him through his boxers and he bucks into my hand.

I take him out of his boxer briefs and his dick stands at attention pointing straight up all rigid and strong and veiny. I clench my thighs, wishing he could be inside me, but sadly that's not an option. So I lean forward and take him in my mouth.

His hands move to my hair and I do everything he loves. The lollipop swirl, the deep throat, the sucking and jerking off, my hand on his balls. I use all my best moves. The ones that make him say my name like a prayer. The ones that make his words almost inaudible. The ones where he grips my strands so tight my scalp tingles.

Long forgotten are the issues of the tuxedo or the worries about the rehearsal dinner, which I know is the underlying problem because he's nervous to cook for that many people all at once and he wants to impress his friends and family. But I trust him. Besides, we have so much going on in life right now we have to take a time out and remember what matters most in this world is us. Us. Our family. The soon-to-be Baileys.

He comes with a jolt and I swallow, licking him clean. "Better?" I ask, resting my chin on his thigh.

"I wish I could repay you."

"I'm good." I crawl into his lap and he kisses my neck.

"You sure? I can be gentle." His hands run up my chest and he squeezes my breast, and a small amount of milk leaks onto my shirt. "It's kinda hot watching this."

"Um, this is how your child is eating right now."

"I just want to be buried inside of you." He slides me closer, his breath heavy in my ear and his tongue swirling around my earlobe.

"Me too, but I'm not in any condition right now."

"Post-pregnancy sucks."

I laugh and Dion stirs, a small whine floating out of him.

"You go rest. I'll be on daddy duty for a while."

"I love you," I say, climbing off his lap. "The bottles are in the fridge."

He shoots me a look to say he knows how to care for his son.

But as much as I want sex, sleep sounds like winning the mega millions right now. So I go to the bedroom with the monitor for Calista.

I WAKE up to the sound of Calista whining about something. Bolting up, I look toward the window and see the sun low in the sky. Without even looking I can tell I've been asleep for a while, my breasts are engorged and sore.

"Shit!" I run out of the room to find Rome with Dion in the sling attached to him playing a game of kitchen with Calista. She's dressed and out of her pajamas although Rome is still wearing his, which means he slept too.

"Why didn't you wake me?" I come over to them, kissing each one of my loves.

"You needed the sleep. You were out cold."

My head falls to his shoulder. "Thank you. Right now that's better than an orgasm."

He chuckles. "Glad I can satisfy you in *and* out of bed."

Calista hangs up the pretend phone she's speaking to someone on and hands Rome a plastic hot dog and a milk carton.

"Want me to take him?" I say.

He stares down at Dion. "I fed him using some of the milk from the freezer."

"You're the best." I can't help the smile that pulls at the corner of my lips.

He glances down at his chest. "I understand this wrap thing now. Gives you use of both hands."

I nod and smile, taking in this man who never ceases to surprise me at how adaptable he can be.

My phone rings on the counter and I walk over to grab it.

"It's been going off all evening, but I told them I wasn't waking you up."

I pick up my phone to see thirty-four missed messages in the Bailey girl group message.

"What's wrong?" I ask him because to hell if I want to read thirty-four messages.

He meets my gaze. "As of right now, the wedding's off."

"What?" I yell so loud, Dion cries.

Rome soothes him with a rocking motion and a few rubs down his small back.

"Relax, it's all so stupid. They'll figure it out."

8

———

Austin

Two days before the wedding...

I ring the doorbell to Liam's house. Visiting Jack wasn't an option since Frannie would lecture about how walking out on Holly in the middle of an argument right before our wedding wasn't my most brilliant idea. I know it's not, but we needed a bit of space before things got heated.

The stress of the wedding has gotten to both of us. Case in point? She blew up when I refused to postpone our honeymoon to coach my team at state. Holly is always a little high strung, but this wedding has put her in the red zone for the past few weeks.

"Well, it's not a celebration unless someone's gotta kiss ass." Liam opens the door. His clothes are covered in sweat and he has a green smoothie in hand.

"I just need to lie low for a while."

"I'm not sure this is the place but c'mon in." He opens the door wider and I step in, heading to the kitchen and finding Savannah in her pajamas sitting at the breakfast bar.

Her eyes leave her laptop and she glances over.

Liam's place resembles a log cabin. The kind you find at the bottom of ski hills, not in the backwoods. It's mostly all wood with a rustic feel. Somehow as sophisticated as Savannah is, she fits in this space.

"I heard you made a dip shit move," my sister says.

Liam leaves me to go pour me a cup of coffee and puts it on the breakfast bar next to Savannah.

"I told her I was fine with missing the game."

"But are you really?" Savannah asks. She crosses her legs and it's then that I notice her matching pajamas. When she lived with me, she wore boxer shorts and old t-shirts. What's up with that?

Forget it. None of my business and I don't want to know if she's trying to impress Liam or not. I can only deal with one crisis at a time.

"Yes, I really am fine with it. It's our wedding. Our honeymoon. We only get one. This might sound dickish, but when the team won regionals, I was surprised. It's not something I planned, but it doesn't change that she comes first in my life."

"That's a wise decision. I mean, what woman wouldn't be offended." Liam takes off his shirt and wipes off sweat from his stomach.

I turn to Savannah to get her take. She's been my female drama fix-it girl forever. She's staring at Liam.

"Sav?"

She blinks and then her eyes transform to lasers. "I'm sure Holly understands the predicament you're in, and if you would've listened to her instead of being hell-bent on proving some point, you'd be at your own house right now."

Denver stumbles into the kitchen. "What the hell? I'm used to dealing with that one waking up early, but you too?" He points at Savannah. "All I could hear is your angry typing on the keyboard."

Savannah gives him her bored look and circles back my way to continue to make her point. But the door to the house opens and in comes Rome, one hand pulling Calista along and the other on the baby carrier strapped to his front. Calista's holding a box of donut holes and has powdered sugar all over her face.

"We're here to save the day," Rome says.

Calista laughs, putting on her best Supergirl act. Something I'm sure her daddy taught her to do before they walked in.

"I don't need everyone here." I run a hand through my hair, processing what Savannah said. Maybe she's right. Ever since I almost boarded that plane like an idiot to leave Holly, I've tried to make sure she knows where she stands in my life—number one.

"Oh, come on. The girls are all getting together," Rome says.

I look to Savannah. She nods. Without me even having to ask the question in my head, she answers. "I told them I'd stay since I'd be the only one here to talk some sense into you."

I don't argue her point, but Liam shakes his head.

Rome covers his heart and falters back like I shot him.

Denver, well, he's standing with the fridge door wide open, staring inside and scratching his chest while still trying to wake up.

"Unless you want to chip in for the electric bill, shut it," Liam says.

"I pay rent."

"You really wanna go there?" Liam deadpans.

Denver pulls out a small bottle of orange juice and shuts the fridge, rolling his eyes in a dramatic fashion. He'll eventually have to find somewhere to live on a permanent basis.

"Savannah had that make-your-hair-flat thing plugged in most of the day yesterday," Denver says, twisting the top off his drink.

"It turns itself off," she says.

"When?" He holds up his hand. "It burned me."

"I warned you before I left for work," she snips.

"Can we please talk about my problem right now?" I interrupt the sibling fight.

Calista climbs up on Savannah's lap and offers her a donut hole, holding it up to her lips.

"Oh no. Thank you though, sweetie."

"Auntie." Calista displays her pouty face and Savannah opens her mouth. Instead of letting Savannah bite down on it, Calista sticks the entire thing into her mouth, surprising Savannah.

We all laugh. Liam reaches over for a napkin and hands it to Savannah. She nods a thank you and I'm actually impressed by how civil they are to one another.

"Feed me, baby girl?" Rome sticks his head between the two of us with his wide mouth open.

"Maybe you should lay off the sweets," Denver says.

Rome flips him off behind his daughter's back, but takes the donut, acting like he's eating her fingers.

"Daddy!" Calista erupts into a fit of giggles.

I watch the interaction and I know it's weird, but my

heart fills with envy. I want what my brother has, and I want it with Holly.

"I'm guessing this is some stupid fight?" Rome says.

"Fight?" Denver asks.

"The wedding's off," Rome says.

Savannah, Liam, and I all turn to Rome. "It's not off."

He shrugs like 'oh, my bad.'

"We're arguing, but it's not off," I say.

"I figured there was another fight between Liam and Sav or something." Denver downs his orange juice.

"I think Uncle Denver wants one." Savannah takes one from the box. "Here you go." She throws it at him.

He catches it in his mouth and winks at Calista. Her eyes widen like he's her favorite Disney character and she takes one from the box and throws another one. He catches it in his mouth again. We'll be here all day.

When she picks up a third, Denver shakes his head still chewing the first two. "I gotta watch my figure, not like your daddy."

Rome reaches in and throws one, catching him off guard. It hits Denver in the forehead and drops into his lap. He picks it up and eats it.

"Stop with the jokes," Rome says.

"Go for a run," Denver counters.

"If my kids weren't here, I'd throw down with you."

Savannah and I share a look because this was what our life was like once upon a time, but we're all too fucking old to break up their fights now.

"Anyway," Sav says loudly, getting everyone's attention. "Go to her. Talk to her. Tell her that you appreciate the fact that she delayed the honeymoon, and you humbly accept, but that it doesn't mean baseball takes priority over her." Savannah touches my arm.

Liam snorts.

"What?" She whips her head in his direction.

"It's just interesting that you're able to make so much sense and see things so clearly when it comes to other people's love lives." Liam crosses his ankles and presses his hands behind him on the counter.

"I don't have a love life," she admits, which I know upsets her. But the guys Savannah goes for don't live in a small town like Lake Starlight.

"Exactly," Liam says, face void of emotion.

"You're right. I should talk to her. Clear this up and make sure she knows I'm not angry at her for delaying our honeymoon. I still have the whole issue of her dad to deal with though."

"She wants that asshole there?" Savannah asks.

"I'll be her bodyguard," Denver raises his hand. "Rome's got his hands full now."

Savannah shoots him an expression as if to say, 'go to hell.' "Why would she want him there?" she asks.

"Because he's her dad," Liam says matter-of-factly.

Savannah turns to Liam and nods. I exchange a look with Denver like did she actually agree with him?

"I'm fine if he comes. Tell her whatever she wants is fine and I promise to keep my cool," she says.

"I'm sure between me and Denver, we can make sure he doesn't get close enough to her to be able to aggravate her," Liam says and that mutual respect thing from moments ago disappears. Savannah looks sour.

"Do what you want. I'm going to spend some time with my niece and nephew."

"Perfect. Here." Rome hands her Dion.

Savannah takes the baby in her arms and tells Calista to go get her bag of toys. I'm sure people would be surprised about Savannah's maternal instincts, but truth is, she helped raise six younger siblings. She was our mom's helper even before her death, so she knows what she's doing.

Rome sits down where Sav was and looks at the computer screen. "What's this?" he asks.

Denver rounds the counter and I lean over.

"It's just work," Savannah yells out. "Shut it."

It looks like a pro and con list of some kind, but Rome shuts it and slides it away before I get a good look.

"Buzzkill. Fatherhood isn't boasting well for you."

"Denver, stop the razzing." My own fatherly tendencies shine through when the twins go at it. Denver won't let this weight thing with Rome go and pretty soon there's going to be a fight and I can't have that at my wedding.

I knock on the counter. "I'm out. I have to go make up with Holly."

"Good idea," Liam says. Sometimes I wonder why he seems so much more mature than my brothers who are the same age.

"Thanks, Savannah." I wave and she waves back, rocking Dion in her arms while spinning something for a game with Calista. She can definitely multi-task like a mother.

9

———

Savannah

Rome leaves with Denver, making some sly remark about buying a jogging stroller.

"Rome is going to kick his ass soon," I remark, shutting the door to Liam's house.

He's cleaning up the kitchen and I go in to pick up my computer off the breakfast bar.

"I know. Hopefully Denver's over his jokes before the wedding otherwise, I fear the cake table might collapse when those two go at it." Liam would be a man after my own heart. He's wiping down the counters and cleaning out the blender from his smoothie. He's neat, and I begrudgingly like that about him.

"Maybe I should say something."

He turns off the water, grabs a paper towel to dry his hands. "No, you have enough to deal with. I'll do it."

"Thanks."

My stomach is still queasy with the thought of seeing Holly's dad. Hate isn't a strong enough word for how I feel about that man, but it's her dad and Liam was right, my issues with him need to be put aside for the day.

"Who should I bet on?"

"What?" I ask, holding my laptop to my chest.

"You and Holly's dad or Rome and Denver?"

"I can control myself."

He leans against the counter, crossing his arms over his chest. He's such a cocky son of a bitch. "You have a hard time with me. Why is that?"

"Do we really have to do this now?"

"We have the house to ourselves. Why not?"

I blow out a breath and sit on the stool. "We're just very different people."

He studies me for a second and I have no idea what he wants from me. Pushing off the counter, he throws the paper towel in the garbage. "I'll be in the barn." He never looks back at me and exits through the backdoor.

"Liam," I sigh, but I'm too late. The screen door slams shut, and my head falls back to stare up at the ceiling. I don't even know what he does in that barn of his. Probably where his gym is, which explains why every morning I'm tortured with having to see him all sweaty from his work-out.

Jeez, I haven't had sex in way too long if I'm getting excited over perspiration.

My phone dings and I grab it off the charger.

JUNO: **Well?**

Me: He's on his way to Holly.

Juno: Good job. Way to go.

.   .   .

I GRAB my phone and head upstairs to get ready for the day, trying to forget Liam Kelly and what his abs do to my libido.

DRIVING up to North Forest Lumber Company in Sunrise Bay brings a sourness to my stomach, but I'm a good sister-in-law and I love Holly. I want her day to be everything it should be and more.

I park my SUV and stare at the building of Bailey Lumber's biggest competitor and enemy. I hate everything about him and this company. He tried to take us down with rumors and lies and I haven't forgotten it.

Just go in. Just go in. I tell myself over and over again until I finally open the door and step out of my car. There's still a nip in the air which as far as I'm concerned is perfect for a beautiful wedding because no one will be sweating their asses off.

I cross the parking lot and open the glass doors, finding no receptionist. Looking around, I head down the hallway in search of someone who can point me in the right direction.

When I enter the main area, an open concept space with cubicles and phones ringing off the hook but no one is answering them.

"Excuse me." I stop a guy who has a bunch of papers in his hands. "Can you point me to Clint Edison's office?"

"You're kidding me, right?"

I tilt my head. "Um... no."

"He skipped town. He was embezzling funds from the company."

"What?"

He nods and moves along down the hall. This has got to

be a joke. Why wouldn't I have heard about this? We're in the same industry.

I stop another employee, a woman this time, with the hopes that she feels like being chatty enough to give me the lowdown.

"When did they find out Clint Edison was embezzling?" She looks at me and then I see the recognition in her eyes.

"Savannah Bailey?"

I nod.

She looks around and ushers me back toward the reception area where no one else is.

"I shouldn't be telling you this, but the investors figured it out anyway. We all kind of knew something was going on for months. He was firing and laying off employees weekly and then today, one of the partners came in and told us all what was happening."

I soak in the information. My mind should be on Holly and not on how well this will work for Bailey Timber, but I prayed for years that the world would see what a slimeball that guy really is.

"I'm sorry," I say, meaning it because this means a lot of people are out of a job.

"Well, if you have any openings." She looks at me hopefully.

"What's your name?" I ask.

"Grace Holden."

I put my hand out. "Call my office Monday morning, Grace and I'll see what I can do."

"Thanks." She looks behind her and I get the idea that I should probably leave before anyone else sees me, so I head out, my mind a jumbled mess.

It takes me a half hour to get to Austin and Holly's place. Both of their vehicles are parked in the driveway. On the way over here I was hoping it'd only be Austin so that he could break the news to Holly himself.

I ring the doorbell which I'm still getting used to doing since it is my childhood home. I hear Myles' paws along the hardwood floors they had installed. Long gone is the horrible carpet we never upgraded.

"Calm down," Austin says to the dog from behind the door.

Shock morphs his features when he sees it's me. "Sav?"

"Everything good?"

He nods. "Yeah, we'll all good. We're delaying the honeymoon until after the state tournament. I did push back though, and we'll be extending our time away for another week." He opens the door wider for me, and I step in, taking off my shoes.

Myles slobbers all over my hands and I pet him hello. Daisy comes around the corner, her tail wagging.

"Who is it?" Holly asks from the kitchen.

"We're making dinner. You want to join?" Austin asks.

"Um... no. This is your last night before the wedding stuff really gets underway. I just came here to tell you about some information I came upon."

He tilts his head.

"It's about Holly's dad."

Austin's shoulders fall. "Austin?" Holly calls out since he didn't answer her question the first time.

"It's Sav."

"Come in, Savannah. Sorry about earlier." Her voice grows closer and I have no opportunity to tell Austin before Holly joins us. My gut twists watching her smile.

"No need. I understand how Austin can be at times."

She giggles and Austin walks over to her and kisses her head. "Savannah has information about your dad."

Her smile fades and I guess there's no easing into it now.

"What?" She shakes her head. "Do I need a drink? Come in. Let's grab a drink."

She disappears and I follow her, Austin between us. He grabs two wine glasses and a bottle of Holly's favorite white wine from the fridge.

"Thanks."

"Want to go outside? It's beautiful outside right now." Holly picks up her wine glass and opens the screen door.

"Babe?" Austin says, and Holly stops, turning back around.

Her expression says it all. She knows she's about to be disappointed and hoped that maybe she could delay it. She sits down next to me and seems to brace herself. "Okay. What is it?"

I gather my thoughts in my head so I do a good job of delivering this blow. "I went to ask your dad to come to the wedding. I didn't want you not to have him there because of me."

"What?" She looks to Austin.

"Well?" he says.

"You weren't the reason I didn't invite him, Savannah. I know you would've tried to hold it together."

"You have more faith in me than my brothers."

She laughs. "Well, they're men."

"True. Anyway, I went there, and I found out he was gone. I guess he was embezzling from the company and now the partners are looking for him. I think he fled."

She stares at me like she cannot wrap her head around it. "Oh. Well, I shouldn't be surprised, I guess." She stares down at her wine glass for a minute, deep in thought." What about his family?"

I shrug. "I don't know. I assume they're with him. Or that the wife was blindsided."

She looks to Austin and he comes over to her, putting his arm around her shoulders. Just as we're figuring out what to do, the five o'clock news comes on the television in the family room.

We all move in there to watch it.

"Local business owner, Clint Edison, embezzled over three-hundred thousand dollars from his company. He was found at the airport, flying alone. His wife of Sunrise Bay says she didn't know anything, but evidence shows the contrary. They have three kids who are in the mother's care tonight while Edison awaits to appear in front of a judge."

A picture of the building I was just at flashes across the screen.

Holly continues watching even though the segment is over. "It's so weird. I feel like I should have all these feelings and I don't. I hope the kids and his wife end up okay, but…"

Austin pulls her to him and kisses her forehead. I figure my time is up, so I wave goodbye to Austin and slide out the front door.

I'm not beside my truck checking my phone for more than a minute when the door opens, and Holly runs out to me with Myles on her heels. Austin waits at the door with Daisy.

"Savannah," she says, rushing over to me, both her arms swathing me in a hug. "Thank you."

"For what? Giving you bad news two days before your wedding?"

She draws back. "That you would have sat through the wedding with him there for my happiness. You know it's amazing that non-blood relationships can be worth more than blood sometimes. You're more family to me than Clint

Edison ever was. Thank you." She hugs me one more time. This time tighter and longer.

"We love you, Holly. You're a Bailey."

She wipes her tears and smiles. "That means so much."

"Now go in there and enjoy your last night living in sin."

She laughs through her tears. "Will do."

"I'll see you tomorrow."

She starts to walk away. "You will."

I climb into the SUV and she waits with Austin on the porch, waving goodbye as I drive down their long driveway to the other side of town. The ache between my legs only intensifying as I get closer to Liam's.

10

Holly

The day before the wedding...

Terra and Mare is decorated with rows of tea lights in the centers of the long tables extending the width of the restaurant. Flower petals are scattered along the wood surface and their scent lingers in the air.

Rome walks out of the back wearing his chef's jacket.

"Rome, it's beautiful."

He leans forward and kisses my cheek. "Let's just hope the food tastes good."

"I'm sure it will be delicious."

All of our groomsmen and bridesmaids start to arrive since we came here right after the rehearsal for the ceremony. Grandma Dori is at the bar ordering herself a beer. Harley comes in through the back with Dion in a stroller and Calista looks adorable in her sundress and sandals. Harley is such an awesome mom, I'll never compare.

"Have you seen Liam?" Savannah asks me.

I look around. Weird. He was just at the rehearsal.

"He had to go pick up his date," Denver says, joining our conversation.

You know when you're somewhere loud and everything around you just stops and becomes still and quiet? That's what happens now. Even Dion's cries die down.

"You need something? You know I'm stronger than him anyway." Is Denver the only one not noticing that it's weird that Liam would bring a date? He never brings a date to anything.

"Does Liam have a girlfriend?" I ask for Savannah's sake because I owe her one after what she tried to do for me last night.

"Liam? Hell no." Denver scrunches his face up.

"Denver." Harley points to Calista who is busy staring up at her uncle like he's the life-size version of Superman.

"Sorry." He cringes. "But Liam's a loner for life."

"What the hell are you talking about?" Austin says.

"I need to see Rome. His selection of beer is not up to my standards." Grandma Dori joins our little circle.

"What are you looking for?" Harley says, pulling Dion out of the stroller.

Juno comes in and swoops him up in her arms. Her and Phoenix and Sedona all head to a table far away from everyone with both the kids.

"I love this big family thing." Harley smiles and releases a breath.

"He doesn't have Coors or Miller or Bud."

"He has Stella," Harley says, trying to appease her.

"He has beers I've never heard of. Fancy beers. Frou-frou beers."

"You should try Stella," Denver says.

She puts her hand on Denver's shoulder. "Go down to Liquory Split and get me a six of Miller."

Denver shakes his head but leaves the restaurant to fulfill his grandmother's request.

Austin kisses my cheek and says he'll be back. Grandma Dori moves around the room like a politician waiting for her lackey to bring her beer.

"Can you believe it?" Brooklyn rushes over, poking her head between me and Savannah. The three of us huddle together.

"What?" I ask.

"He hasn't proposed yet," she says.

Yesterday morning, Brooklyn let all the women know that she found a ring in Wyatt's stuff. Now she's on pins and needles every time she thinks it's the perfect opportunity to propose. She's going to combust if he doesn't do it soon.

"It could be awhile. You need to chill. You just moved in together. You have chickens," Savannah, always the voice of reason says.

"Yeah, that's true. Those things are hard work. It's like having babies, I swear."

"You don't really know what having a baby is like," Savannah kindly reminds her as an exhausted Harley rejoins us. She looks presentable, but you can tell she's not really all there if you look into her eyes. Her gaze keeps moving back and forth to the babies.

"What about babies?" she asks.

"Nothing," I say because Harley will speak her mind and Brooklyn's casual comparative might not be well received right now.

Harley rolls her shoulders and moves her neck around in a circular motion like it's too heavy to hold up. "I swear after-pregnancy sucks more than when you're pregnant. At least when you're pregnant, you have a reason to not drink. I can't have sex, I can't drink, I'm being used like a world fair's champion cow for milk supply." She looks like she might tear up.

"What could be taking him so long? Is it because I was already engaged before, do you think?"

"No," Savannah says.

"Are we talking about the ring thing?" Harley asks.

"Yeah," Savannah and I say in unison.

"When the time is right, he'll ask," I say.

"Ask what and who?" Wyatt interrupts the conversation and we all look at one another trying to be discreet, but we're not at all.

"Here you go, G'Ma D!" Denver walks in and raises the case of beer in his hand. "No food yet?"

"Rome's working on it," Harley says and from her expression, I'd say she's not happy with Denver, but maybe it's a hormone thing.

"He's probably sampling too much. Tell me, Harley, are you under that belief that a fat husband is a happy husband?" Denver laughs.

The rest of us remain quiet because Rome just came out with a tray of food. He places it in the middle of the table.

Harley pokes Denver in the chest. "Listen. Rome has gained weight, I'll give you that, but you want to know why?" Denver says nothing and neither do any of us. "See those kids. Your niece and your nephew?"

Denver actually turns and we all sigh.

"He's too busy being a rock star dad to get to the gym much. He's too busy running out and making sure every craving I had during pregnancy was met because guess what? I was growing a human being inside my body. A human being that was half his. He did the stand-up thing and took care of his girlfriend. He's not at the gym doing "curls for the girls" and out partying every night. He's being a true man and taking care of his family and if he's gained a few pounds because of it, I don't care. He's a shit-ton sexier than you." She pokes him in the chest one more time and he holds up his hands.

"I'm sorry. We joke. It's what we do."

Rome comes over and shoves Denver out of his way, picking up Harley and kissing her. It's so romantic how she came to his defense and how he appreciates it.

"Jesus, I was just joking. I didn't mean it." Denver looks over to us and we roll our eyes. One day he'll grow up. I still think he harbors some jealousy that Harley took Rome away and he's going to nit-pick the one thing that isn't perfect between them.

"Girls, you good?" He points to Juno, Phoenix, and Sedona. Sedona is now holding Dion and Phoenix is coloring with Calista. We've yet to figure out why Phoenix came back early with all her bags. She's kind of a 'wait for her to come to you' kind of girl.

Harley and Rome disappear into the kitchen and the serving staff bring out more appetizers, passing them around.

Austin comes and stands next to me, kissing my temple and I slide into his hold, never a better place. My eyes veer over to Dion as guests keep wandering over to get a glimpse of the baby. My hand falls to my stomach. I wonder how long it will take us to get pregnant.

The door opens to the restaurant and after the scene of Denver and Harley, I feel like we're in for round two, except this one will be a quiet boxing round with only scathing looks and cutting verbal remarks.

Liam walks in with a brunette's hand in his. I don't recognize her, but that doesn't mean someone else here doesn't.

He stops, his gaze falling to Savannah.

Why are they doing this to themselves?

I glance over at Savannah and her narrowed eyes are glued to the couple. Anger igniting in them like the quick flame of a gas burner.

"How nice. He brought a date." The tone of her voice is less than convincing.

Liam walks farther into the room and Grandma Dori is the first to stop him. She puts her hand out in front of the woman, shaking her hand. The two weave by her and before too long they're in front of all of us.

"This is Myra," Liam says it like we should all be happy to meet her. I can't be the only Bailey that sees what's going on.

"Hey, Myra. Welcome." My dense husband-to-be puts his hand out first. We all shake and somehow, Savannah is the last one.

"This is Savannah." Liam holds his arm out and Savannah smiles sweetly and extends her hand.

"It's nice to meet you. Have you and Liam been dating long?"

Myra looks to Liam. "No. It's new."

"That's great." Savannah is way too polite.

But we have no time to dwell on them because smoke wafts from out of the kitchen into the restaurant and the smoke alarm goes off.

Harley and Rome run out. Rome's pants are down to his knees. Harley's shirt is off by one button.

They run over to their kids and once Harley has them both and is rushing them out the door, Rome runs back into the kitchen.

The rest of us scramble to leave.

"Maybe you should stay out of the kitchen when Rome's in there," Liam says to Harley. "Seems you're a bit of a distraction."

She looks at him over her shoulder and her cheeks heat.

Savannah just rolls her eyes at Liam's comment and pushes her way past him and his date. I take a deep breath and follow her out. This is life with the Bailey's, but I wouldn't change it for anything.

As we all stay outside the restaurant waiting to be allowed back in by the fire department, I wonder what else could go wrong before my wedding. I inhale a calming breath reminding myself that as long as I become Mrs. Austin Bailey, it will all be fine.

Eventually, Li from Wok For U comes around the corner carrying bags of food.

"Li!" Austin screams.

"Rome told me you needed some food."

We set up an impromptu picnic in the gazebo in the square.

"I'm sorry you two." Rome walks over, looking humbled.

"Hey, orange chicken was our first meal together." I stare up at Austin and he smiles, leaning down to kiss me.

"Thanks for understanding."

"How's the damage?" Austin asks him.

"Minimal in the kitchen, but insurance claim here I come." He runs his hand on my back. "Sorry."

"It's fine."

As I lean along Austin's chest, we stare at our guests laughing and enjoying themselves in their dresses and nice clothes sitting on the grass.

"These are for you two." Li hands Austin two fortune cookies.

"Thanks." Austin holds them out for me, and I grab one, cracking it open.

"Marriage lets you annoy one special person for the rest of your life." I laugh and he kisses me.

Austin cracks his open. "And they lived happily ever after."

"I didn't need a fortune to know that." I smile up at my soon-to-be husband then stuff my end of the fortune cookie into his mouth.

He tightens his arms around my stomach. "We got this in spades, baby."

"I love you," I whisper.

"I love you more."

11

———

Liam

Day of the wedding

"The florist isn't here," Savannah says to us when Denver and I climb out of the car.

It'd be a lot easier to act indifferent to her if she didn't look so goddamn hot. She has one shoulder bare and her hair is pulled up off her neck into some hairstyle that I really don't care about. What I do care about is the curve of her neck and how much my mouth would enjoy tasting her there.

"Did you go to the shop? It's like thirty feet away," Denver says.

"No Denver, I didn't. I run a huge company, but the idea that I should swing by her shop didn't cross my mind."

"Where's the bride?" I ask. We don't have time for these two to bicker if we're going to fix this problem.

"She's with the other bridesmaids. Dana is keeping her distracted," Savannah says.

I look to the gazebo and see that it's bare, nothing distinguishing it from being any other day. There have been multiple weddings here in the past, my parents included, and it's usually done to the nines.

"Let me call Faith." I pull out my phone.

"You have the florist's phone number?" Sav asks.

I grin over at her. "Ah, don't be jealous. Her shop's two doors down from mine."

Savannah looks away. I like her jealous, which is why I brought Myra to the rehearsal dinner. It was a shitty move on my part, but I have to do what I have to do. So does she, I suppose.

"Why would Sav be jealous?" Denver asks. I swear he's blind. "Not to mention isn't Faith a friend of your mom's?"

I hold up my finger when Faith picks up. "Hey Faith, it's Liam. I'm at the Bailey wedding and the flowers aren't up yet."

She tells me she caught something and that she left a message earlier for Holly. All the flowers are in her cooler, ready to go, but she can't get here.

"Do you mind if I come by and get the key?"

Savannah looks up at me with wide eyes while Faith agrees.

"I'll be right over. Thanks." I tuck my phone into my tux pants. "I'm going to pick up her key and we can grab the flowers from her cooler, then the three of us can put them up."

"Us? She was hired to do a job," Savannah says.

"And she got sick. Life happens, we adjust," I say.

She says nothing and the three of us climb into my car, Savannah calling shotgun and taking the front seat.

"This is bullshit," Denver says, climbing into the back.

"I think you've spoken enough the past few days. You're pissing everyone off." Savannah turns around and gives him a look, but it's true though. Denver needs to get whatever is wrong with him out in the open because it's festering and ruining his relationship with his twin brother.

"So is Myra coming to the wedding?" Savannah crosses her legs and God help me there's a large slit in her dress showcasing her legs. Long legs in a pair of fuck-me heels.

"No," I croak out because my brain is busy processing my next beat off reel.

"Why not?"

"I'm not sure it's going to work out." I turn up the volume.

She leans forward and turns it down.

"Sav, I love that song," Denver whines from the backseat.

"That's a shame," Savannah says.

"Is it?" I ask her with an eyebrow raised.

"Yes."

I shrug. "Okay."

A low growl escapes her, and I want to laugh because she's so easy to get a rise out of. It's ridiculous how much I get under her skin.

Luckily, Faith lives near downtown, so we get there fast, and I run up to her door to get the key.

We're back in downtown Lake Starlight before we can have another uncomfortable conversation. Good thing too because I'm close to not giving a shit that her brother is in the backseat and deciding to take her anyway.

The three of us get to the cooler, and we quickly send Denver to deliver the bouquets to the girls. Savannah calls Kingston and he takes the boutonnieres, leaving us with the decorations for the gazebo.

"I'm not a creative person," she admits like I haven't cataloged almost every single thing about her over the years.

"I know."

"Thanks," she deadpans.

"We all have our good attributes. I knew creativity wasn't your thing when I ran into you at Lucky's that night you tried a wine and painting class."

"Again, thank you." She struggles with the giant white buckets that hold the flowers to be arranged along the posts.

"I couldn't do a spreadsheet," I admit, trying to make her feel better.

"You're not creative, are you?" she asks, staring up at the gazebo with trepidation.

I'm insulted, but of course she only sees me as some dirtbag tattoo artist. "I don't know. How's the blackbird tattoo on your hip bone?"

"I know you can draw, but this is flower arrangement."

"Technically we're just installing them."

"Why are you so frustrating?" Another growl runs up her throat. "You're so trying."

"I could say the same." I always keep my voice even-keeled when with Savannah because it aggravates her even more. I don't always want to piss her off, but she's the one playing the games right now.

"Let's just do this." She takes one of the arrangements out and we decide together that we'll put one on every other post. Then she takes the loose petals and scatters them up the stairs.

We head back to Faith's and get the stakes that hold the candles and flowers at the end of each row of chairs. I abide by her wishes and remain quiet the whole time. No need for us to talk about anything.

"Do you miss your parents?" she asks out of the blue.

I guess I shouldn't be too surprised she's asking. Parents have been a topic of conversation a lot this week in town. The first Bailey wedding and the parents' chairs will be empty. There's a memorial area set up and flowers will sit in the seats that would've been for Mr. and Mrs. Bailey if they'd been alive to witness their firstborn marry the woman he loves.

"Yeah. I go down and visit once a year," I say.

"They rarely come back," she says, working the flowers along the poles at the end of the chair rows.

I turn to see that she just laid the flowers down on her parents' chairs, which I'm guessing is what spurred this conversation.

"Traveling isn't their thing." I shrug.

"You stayed all these years after they left."

"Is there a question in there?" I delay answering because there are reasons I stayed but none that she'd care to hear.

"Why?"

I meet her gaze for a moment then get back to work arranging the flowers in my hands. "This is my life. This is where I grew up. I wanted to build my business and my life here. My friends are here. I love Lake Starlight."

She's silent for so long that I finally look over at her to find a stunned expression on her face.

"What?" I ask.

"You've never spoken that many sentences to me before without there being animosity."

I chuckle. "Well, I guess there's a first for everything."

"Yeah, I suppose."

More silence commences in the gazebo, the only noise coming from the cars slowly driving past.

"Do you miss them?" I ask.

I hear her deep inhale and I kind of wish I could have kept my need-to-know-where-her-heads-at to myself.

She sits down on a chair. "Days like today are hard. They've missed so many milestones." She takes her finger and blots her eye. "Damn, I'm going to ruin my makeup."

I take the seat next to her and grab the handkerchief out of the inside pocket of my jacket and hand it to her.

"You carry these?" she asks, taking it from my hand.

"I figured one of you Baileys would need it today. My money was on Rome though."

She smiles and nods. "Thanks."

"Sure thing."

"I'm just stressed," she says. "I'm always so stressed," she says a little quieter.

"I could help you with that." I smile and she shakes her head, but there's a smile there too.

"I know we don't always see eye to eye but if you ever need me or—"

"Finally, you two. We've been waiting for you guys," Sedona interrupts from behind. "Oh, it looks beautiful! You guys make a great team."

I stand and offer my hand to Savannah. She hands me back my handkerchief and stands on her own. "Thanks," she mumbles and walks with her sister to Rome's apartment where all the girls are getting ready.

I head to Terra and Mare where all the guys are.

My eyes stay trained on her and she glances over her shoulder at me.

That woman's mind is a labyrinth I'll never figure out.

12

———

Austin

I'm in Rome's office reading over my vows when the door opens.

"Just give me like two minutes," I say.

"Are you sure?" Holly's voice has me turning around. "Not yet!" I stop moving before I'm all the way turned around.

The door shuts and the air in the room changes with her in it.

"You don't have to do this. I made peace with it," I say.

"Austin, turn around."

"Really babe, I'm good. Promise."

"Turn around."

"Are you sure?"

"You're ruining the moment." She huffs.

I circle around and take her in. Her hair is pulled back with a veil pinned to the bottom. The white beaded top of her dress highlights her curves showing just a hint of cleavage and the layers of cascading white fabric from the waist down suit her perfectly. She is a vision in white and literally takes my breath away.

"Well?" she asks when I don't say anything.

"You're stunning. So beautiful. Why are you marrying me?"

She laughs and steps forward. "You look very handsome." Her fingers run down my lapels.

"I look like a schmuck compared to you."

"Thank you, but I disagree."

My eyes can't stop soaking in every inch of her. My bride. My soon-to-be-wife. "I can't believe you want to marry me."

"Since the first night at Lucky's."

"You knew then?" I ask.

Her arms loop around my neck. "I haven't put my lipstick on yet."

"Is that an invitation?"

She smiles up at me. "You don't need an invitation, Austin. I'm yours."

"I love it when you say that." I press my lips to hers. This could get carried away quickly if we're not careful.

After our kiss ends, she pulls back slightly. "I snuck out, so I better get back before they think I'm a runaway bride."

I laugh, placing both hands on her cheeks, kissing her one more time. "I'm the luckiest man in the world."

"Well, I'm not going to argue, but I'm pretty lucky too." She turns out of my hold and goes to the door. "Wait for me at the altar?"

"With bated breath."

She smiles and slips out, shutting the door behind her.

Ten minutes later, I'm standing on the top platform of the gazebo. My groomsmen are lined up down each step and wrapping around the side. My heart beats out of my chest and my palms are sweaty.

After I proposed, we contemplated eloping and sometimes I think we should have. Who needs all this planning and the big bill that comes with a wedding like this? But I also wanted to declare my commitment to her publicly. I wanted everyone to know she's mine. Add on the responsibility the Baileys have to this town and it felt necessary to do this here in Lake Starlight. Luckily, Holly agreed.

Now that I look out at all the faces in the audience. I know it was the right decision. I glance at the two chairs occupied only with flower arrangements to signify my parents' love. My Uncle Brian and Grandma Dori sit beside the empty chairs waiting for Karen, Holly's mother.

The music starts and I hold my breath as all my sisters walk down the aisle on their own. Then Calista comes with Harley holding Dion in her arms. Calista places one petal down and stops, places another petal down and stops. If we continue at this rate, we'll be here all night. Harley bends down and whispers in her ear, trying to get her hand in the basket but Calista scowls and shifts it away from her mother.

I hear Rome laugh. "That's my girl. You do you."

Harley shoots me an 'I'm sorry' expression, but I shake my head. My niece can do whatever she wants.

A lifetime later, and after another repeat of the song thanks to the Lake Starlight high school orchestra, the petals are all in place.

Then Frannie walks down the aisle with Myles and Daisy on their leashes. Myles is in a bow tie and Daisy's in a dress she'll probably never keep on. She puts them in the pen we set up so no one would have to hold them the entire time.

The music shifts and Jack elbows me. There stands my beautiful bride at the end of the aisle on her mom's arm. Our eyes catch and she walks forward looking at me the entire way.

My anxiety about today and all the people fades the closer she gets to me.

I kiss Karen on the cheek, and she lifts Holly's veil.

"You're beautiful," I whisper to her.

"Thank you. You ready to make this official?"

"Definitely."

We walk up to the pastor and the ceremony goes off without a hitch. Twenty minutes later we're kissing and holding hands facing all our guests as the pastor announces us. "I now present you, Mr. and Mrs. Bailey."

I walk by my parents' chairs and for a moment I envision them there smiling and clapping, my mom with tears streaming down her cheeks, pure joy for me, their eldest son.

Holly squeezes my hand as though she knows. I smile and stop us in the middle of the row, bending down to kiss her. I truly am the luckiest man in the world.

13

Grandma Dori

My oldest grandchild is married.

I'm so thankful I was still around to see the big day. I sit in the chair at one of the tables on the outskirts of Lake Starlight, settling in and taking stock of all my grandchildren.

Brooklyn and Wyatt dancing together in a loving embrace. She found the ring. Juno let it slip to me and I hope Brooklyn finds the patience to wait until he's ready to propose.

Rome holds Dion with Harley next to him and Calista in between them. An instant family that will probably be the next wedding, although I think they'll probably elope.

Phoenix has a secret, but I'm going to give her time to figure it out before I pry too much.

Denver's busy hitting on the bartender in the corner. I wish he'd follow in his twin's footsteps. He'll be such a wonderful father, but someone will have to come and knock him over the head with love. It will take a special person.

Sedona is in the corner on the phone. She's become distant since venturing to New York. Rarely returns home and I have no idea who or what could be more important than spending time with her family. But like with Phoenix, I'm going to give her a few years to spread her wings before I intervene. Hopefully, I'm still around when it's time to swoop in and help.

Kingston's infectious laugh pulls me away from my thoughts and I find him at a table with Selene's daughter, Stella. I forgot that she's home from school for a few weeks. Must be Selene's guest to the wedding. He looks so happy. Then his friend Curtis puts a drink down in front of Stella and takes the chair next to her, resting his arm on the back of her chair. It's the equivalent of a dog pissing on a tree. Kingston stands up, his smile vanishing from his face, but when he catches me looking, he smacks a smile back on. "Hey, G'Ma D, wanna dance?"

"Thanks honey, but I'm too tired."

He nods and walks over to the bar. How will I ever get all my grandkids where they need to be before I die?

Juno and Colton are trying to stop Myles and Daisy from having sex in the corner. Why those two dogs are here, I'll never understand. I swear, people and their dogs these days.

"Your grandchildren are all so beautiful," Ethel says from next to me.

"I know." I smile.

"But Savannah, she never looks happy." She points and I follow the direction her finger is pointing and realize that I left her out when I was taking inventory of where all my grandchildren are in their lives.

Savannah's sipping a glass of champagne, scrolling

through her phone like she'd rather be anywhere else than here.

"She's hard to figure out. A lot goes on in that brain of hers," I say.

"Hello? Oh, hi Midge," Ethel answers her phone through her hearing aid. I'd be annoyed if I wasn't so concerned about Savannah.

She's my sidekick usually, but this is one situation I'll have to fix on my own.

Liam sits at a table right across from her with a scotch neat and his phone in his hands. His gaze flickers up to Savannah every minute or so.

These two might be my hardest case yet.

I stand up, leaving Ethel to talk to Midge from Arizona. That old bat's been talking about going down there in the summers and staying here in the winter. I told her she was doing it the wrong way, but she didn't understand. I'm too old for wasted breath.

Weaving through the tables, I keep my eyes on Savannah but approach Liam.

"Liam? You haven't asked me to dance?"

He looks up from his phone, but the first thing he does is check if Savannah is still there.

"Of course, Mrs. Bailey. I'd be honored." He stands and offers me his arm.

I ignore Savannah although I'm sure her eyes are on us.

Liam escorts me to the makeshift dance floor and he takes my hand in his respectfully, not like Brooklyn and Wyatt.

"So you like my granddaughter?" I ask before we fully circle around.

"Excuse me?"

Oh, Liam is so polite. Something you'd never expect from a man covered in tattoos.

"My granddaughter." He does the box step, but he's got some swagger like my husband did. If I was younger, he might be able to swing me around the dance floor.

"You have a lot of granddaughters." The humor that's lit in his eyes tells me he's playing a game with me. But I'm the master. Juno might call herself the matchmaker, but she gets those skills from my side of the family.

"There's one in particular that you've enamored from afar for many years. Am I wrong?"

"Do you like to be dipped?" he asks.

"Too old for dipping, but Savannah isn't." I take charge and shift us, so he faces her. "Ask her to dance."

"I wouldn't get yourself in the middle, Dori, it will only end badly." He twirls me so that I'm facing Savannah. She's actively trying to pretend she doesn't care what we're talking about. My poor girl.

"I like the middle. It's my favorite place to be." I smile up to him.

"Be careful who you say that to."

Liam's a hard nut and I guess I have no option but to put him in an uncomfortable situation.

"Savannah," I call out.

She glances up from her phone.

"Don't do it, Dori," Liam says but with no real conviction because he knows as do I, that he wants this to happen, he's just not going to admit it to himself.

"I'm old, this is how I enjoy my last years. You're not going to take that away from me, are you?"

His lips fall to a straight line.

"Come here, Savannah." I wave her over.

She stands and walks over like the good granddaughter she is. I feel half bad that she's falling for my trick.

"What?" she asks.

"Here." I leave Liam and hand him over to her.

Our arms fall and the two stand there on the edge of the dance floor while I walk away.

"Grandma?" she asks.

"Don't lose my spot. I'll be right back," I yell back.

Going to get my purse, Ethel is still talking to Midge, but everyone thinks she's delusional and talking to herself since it's through her new Bluetooth hearing aide.

"Let's go," I whisper.

Calista walks by with Sedona. I dig into my purse and hand her the child safety pops I've been instructed only to give her. Cue rolling my eyes.

"Go get Aunt Savannah and Uncle Liam to dance together," I say to Calista.

She looks to the dance floor.

"What are you doing, Grandma?" Sedona asks.

I wave her off.

"He's not my uncle," Calista, my brilliant great-granddaughter, says. Seriously, like genius IQ level this one.

"Not yet, he's not. Not yet. Now scoot." I hand her the lollipop and she skips down the open path taking both their hands and putting them together. When they still don't dance, she pushes on their butts until they start moving.

"You're dangerous," Sedona says.

"Best to remember that."

Ethel and I walk out with her still talking to Midge about how hot Arizona is. No shit, Sherlock.

14

Wyatt

Three days after the wedding...

Austin and Holly's wedding is over. The majority of the town traveled to go see their Lake Starlight baseball team win state. Brooklyn and I are still here because the chickens can't be left alone, but I think that's more of a blessing.

"So, what do you have planned tonight?" She hops up on the counter as I'm making myself a sandwich for lunch. She's been peppy and perky since the wedding.

"Nothing. Want to watch an Avengers movie?"

"Avengers?" she cringes.

"Do you want to watch something else?"

"I was thinking we could go out to eat. Maybe get some wine or a fancy dessert."

Does she really think I'm an amateur at this? Technically, I am. I've never asked a woman to marry me before. But I'm not going to put it in a glass or in a dessert for her to choke on. Total cliché.

She doesn't know that I know she found the ring, but secrets and Baileys never last long. I overheard them talking.

"Let's just get in our pajamas, order a pizza and veg out for the night."

"Oh, okay." She hops off the counter, all pep gone from her step.

"Did you want a sandwich now though?"

"No, I'm not hungry. I'm going to go feed the chickens."

I watch her go to the little coop we built, and she pulls Manhattan out, letting her roam around the yard.

I go upstairs and grab the ring, abandoning my sandwich on the counter. I'd do about anything for this woman, including scrapping my original proposal idea. The proposal doesn't matter, she does.

"Brook? I have to go into town. Want to come with me?" I holler out of the screen door.

"No."

Well, shit.

"Come on. It'll be quick and we can pick up a pie at Lard Have Mercy."

She turns and her lips tip up either because she loves pie, or she thinks I'm going to shove the ring into a blueberry pie. She's wrong. Mostly because there's no errand to go into town for and there's no stopping at Lard.

"Okay." She puts Manhattan back in the coop and walks up to the backdoor like she's a child I just told to come in for the night. "Let me wash my hands."

I swing the keys around my finger, waiting for her, then we go out to my truck. She climbs in without a word. We drive through downtown Lake Starlight, but I don't stop.

"Wyatt, where are you going?"

"I have somewhere else we have to stop first." I head down toward our old apartment complex and park the truck. "Come on." I nod, opening my door.

She meets me in front of the building, and we stare up at where we first met. "No place has ever held happier memories for me than this place." I stare up at her apartment. "From the book that was thrown at my head to when I saw you in a wedding dress standing in front of me."

"What was it you said?" She's playing along.

"I said I thought my worst nightmare had come true."

"Right?" She rolls her eyes. "God forbid you get married."

I swing my arm around her shoulders. "I feel like a different man. Hell, I am a different man. I never knew what I was missing, that when I met the right person, how much my view on it could change."

"It's not like we're married," she says with a tinge of disappointment in her voice.

I shake my head, my left hand digging into my pocket.

"Nope, it's not."

"You can still get out if you want. Yeah, there's the house, but you bought majority."

"When will you understand, it's ours. What's mine is ours."

"I don't have anything to say what's mine is ours."

"Then how about we just be a whole." I open my palm and the sun makes the diamond sparkle even more than it did in the store when I chose it.

"Wyatt!"

I fall down to one knee and hold the ring out for her. "I fell in love with you here in that small apartment and I plan on falling in love with you more every day for the next sixty or more years. How does that sound?"

Her left hand shakes while her right hand covers her mouth. Tears well up in her eyes.

"YES!" she screams, and I slide the ring onto her finger. "This is how it's supposed to feel," she mumbles, and my heart almost bursts I'm so happy.

"Now." I take her in my arms. "Do you have anything to tell me?"

She bites her lower lip and shoots those eyes, that make me do about anything, to me.

"Yes, I know you found the ring. Relieved now?"

"I just love you so much," she says.

I laugh and pull her closer. "The feeling is mutual, my little snoop."

"It was purely by accident."

"You ruined a great proposal."

"Really?"

"You'll never know. It might have been a trip to Paris."

Her eyes bulge. "Was it?"

"Who knows. Let's go home and celebrate."

"Are you thinking big wedding?" she asks as we climb into the truck.

"Whatever you want. I only care that I'm marrying you. We could go somewhere right now if you like. It makes no difference to me."

I start the truck and she touches my hand to stop me from shifting gears.

"Let's do exactly that."

"What?"

"Just go get married. Us two. No one else."

"Now?"

She nods.

"What about the chickens?"

"I'll call Uncle Brian, he didn't go to the game. Couldn't get it off work."

"Okay." I feel my smile inching up at the corners.

"Really?"

I lean over my center console and lay my hand on her cheek. "The sooner you're my wife, the better."

I kiss her and then we drive to the house to pack a bag and go off to secretly get married.

15

———

Myles and Daisy

Three weeks after wedding

Myles flops down next to Daisy by the couch. "They're doing it again."

"I have ears."

"You wanna do it?" he asks her.

"No. I'm not having any more of your puppies. I can barely hold my pee now." Daisy yawns and rolls her head along the blanket.

"They're trying for a baby."

"What are you, the writer of the Lake Starlight Buzzwheel?"

Myles rubs his head to Daisy's. "No, we both know who writes that."

"I was joking." Daisy yawns again.

"They're not going to love us when the baby comes."

"Holly will always love me. You need to stop sniffing that guy's crotch and stop jumping on people if you want to stick around." Daisy's eyes close.

"Let's remember who was here first." Myles turns his head in the other direction.

The iPad lights up on the coffee table and Myles gets on all fours and presses the notification with his nose. A new Buzzwheel post lights up the screen.

We've got a lot of news today....

We have a new Bailey to join our Lake Starlight population count. Holly Bailey has made it official according to the Division of Motor Vehicles. Congratulations to the happy couple.

And a big congratulations again to the Lake Starlight baseball team for winning state. Thankfully everyone was in agreement to wait to have the parade until after the new Mr. and Mrs. Bailey returned from Hawaii. The parade will be this Saturday at ten in the morning. You don't want to miss it.

There's a rumor that we lost a Bailey the same weekend we gained one, but nothing's been changed down at the DMV yet. Brooklyn isn't officially a Whitmore just yet, but we'll see if she decides to change her name.

Have you seen Rome Bailey?? The man is on a mission and we're liking what we see. Someone snapped a picture of him at the gym with his shirt off and let's just say, my dad never looked like that.

Rumors continue to swirl around Savannah Bailey and our hot tattoo artist, Liam Kelly. Nothing is official and no one has any credible evidence that anything is going on with them, but they still have people talking. Who could blame Savannah if she's getting more from Liam than just a house to stay in?

Xo,

    Buzzwheel

COCKAMAMIE UNICORN RAMBLINGS

We're going to be honest with you for a moment. Operation Bailey Wedding was a last minute decision we decided on days before Rome's book, Birth of a Baby Daddy, was about to go live. We never expected the reader's love for The Baileys to be as big as it is when we decided to split the series into three book releases with books from our other world in between. We worried that a drought of five months without a Bailey book would be too long for our readers. And since we aim to please we wanted to give the readers a little something extra and what better way to do that than to write a longer Happily Ever After for the couples in books one through three and to give you a tease into the next Bailey siblings to hit the pages in their own books? Genius, right? :P

How did Brooklyn end up buying chickens?? Rayne's son plays baseball with a boy whose family just got four chickens. She's been hearing the stories from them all summer. Some good, some bad, some cute. And she thought it'd be pretty funny for a city boy like Wyatt to have to deal with chickens.

Thank you to our favorites below who without them, this book isn't possible!

Danielle Sanchez and the entire Wildfire Marketing Solutions team!

Ellie from My Brother's Editor for line edits.

Shawna from Behind the Writer for proofreading.

Sarah from Okay Creations for the cover and branding for the entire series.

Bloggers who consistently carve out time to read, review and/or promote us. It does not go unnoticed and it's not unappreciated.

All the Piper Rayne Unicorns who shout from the rooftops about our new releases and love our characters like we do.

You the readers who took a chance on our book with so many other choices out there.

Obviously, Savannah and Liam are next in line and we can tell you their sexual chemistry is burning up the pages. Don't forget to pre-order your copy for the discounted price so you don't miss out on all the fun!

Xo,

Piper & Rayne

OPERATION

A NOVELLA

PIPER RAYNE

Cover Design: Okay Creations

Editor: Joy Editing

Editor: My Brother's Editor

Proofreader: Shawna Gavas, Behind The Writer

LAKE STARLIGHT BUZZ WHEEL

BUZZ WHEEL PRESS RELEASE: Don't drink the Lake Starlight water! Bailey babies are busy growing in their mommies' tummies and the Baileys are having a triple baby shower to celebrate. If you want in on the pool on who pops first and when, contact me.

$$1$$

Austin

"Motherfu—" I yank out my hand that's being wedged between the back seat and the new car seat.

I'm cramped in the back of Holly's SUV with a car seat jamming into my gut, trying to attach it to two metal prongs hiding in the crease of the seat. Never mind the SATs, they should get high school students to try installing a car seat. If they can figure it out, they're a certified fucking genius in my book.

"You can't use that kind of language when the baby comes," Holly says.

I glance over my shoulder. She's rubbing her swollen stomach behind me, watching with eagle eyes to make sure I get this thing installed just right.

"Good thing she's not here yet," I say.

"Have you thought about those names I gave you yet?"

Thankfully she can't see my face. I love my wife, but I

hate all the names she's come up with. I don't want to name my daughter after a fruit, a tree, a flower, a season, or anything else. Whatever happened to Katie, Kim, or Jennifer? Those are good solid names. But she wants something original. You know, the kind that doesn't even make the top two hundred baby name list kind of name.

"I'm not sure about Reighleigh," I say. "I'd like my daughter to spell her name before she's ten."

The silence behind me is a scary thing. I should've kept my mouth shut.

"Your parents were so original. Why can't we have that?"

"Maybe we should name ours Petri then."

More silence. Guess not.

Holly's lost a little of her sense of humor at this stage of her pregnancy. In the beginning, I think she was so elated about finally becoming pregnant, she took the morning sickness and the fact that she traveled to and from work with her own barf bags like a champ.

Then there are the bouts of melancholy late at night while I'm watching television in bed and she's reading some book she thinks is going to prepare her to become a mother. I'll catch her rubbing and staring at her swollen belly. I'll ask her what's wrong and she'll confess her worry that she'll only experience pregnancy once, so she needs to be sure to really savor this time in her life. Which is part of why I think she's a little grumpier these days. She can't wait to meet our daughter, but it means the end of her pregnancy in just a couple weeks.

"Let's go through the book again," I suggest, crawling out from the back seat after having successfully installed the car seat.

"I wanted a name before the shower so people could have things embroidered or made with her name on it. Juno made sure all of our colors were listed on the invitation if anyone wanted to get personal with their gifts."

"Good thing Savannah and Liam ended up finding out what the sex of the baby is." I rock the seat back and forth to make sure it's secure. How two metal hooks can secure the most precious cargo I'll ever haul, I have no idea.

"How do you think Savannah got him to agree to that?" Holly laughs, leaning in close to inspect whether I did a good job.

I'll admit I was surprised too. Liam had dug his heels in about wanting it to be a surprise and she'd agreed at first. With Savannah's inherent need to control, I thought for sure she'd have everything for the first year of the baby's life ready to go by the time she was six months pregnant. But I think it was all part of her plan—biding her time until she could get him to agree.

"Savannah gets Liam to do a lot of things I'm surprised about."

I slide out of the way because Holly wants me to but doesn't want to seem like she doesn't trust my ability to keep our child safe. It's amazing how you get to know someone's non-verbal communications the longer you're married.

She does the same thing I did with the car seat and inspects all around as though I might have missed something. "Looks good."

I chuckle. "Thanks."

She turns at my laugh. "What?"

"Nothing. Just that she's my daughter too. Do you think I wouldn't make sure she's safe?"

Holly shuts the car door, and I wrap her in my arms. We've mastered the side hug since she hit the third trimester.

"I was just checking," she says.

"Uh-huh."

She swats at my stomach but doesn't look up because she knows exactly what she was doing.

"What do you want for dinner tonight?" I ask.

She shrugs. "Is ice cream an answer?"

Holly told me she'd read that the baby will love what the mother craved during pregnancy. So our baby will probably open an ice cream parlor because Holly only wants ice cream. But only vanilla with candy mixed in.

"Isn't the baby craving steak yet?"

With Holly's aversion to eating a big juicy steak after I grilled some rarer than normal and she saw blood, I've resorted to eating only the Salisbury steak they serve when I visit Grandma Dori at the Northern Lights Retirement Home. The sacrifices we make for the ones we love...

"Sorry."

I nod because missing steak isn't equivalent to carrying a ten-pound bowling ball around in your stomach all day. Holly's doing the heavy lifting here. It was her body that grew bruised and tender from all the shots, her body on the doctor's bed constantly having ultrasounds, her arms poked with a needle every other day to draw blood. She's been through hell for us to have a baby, so if I don't eat steak for the rest of my life, it's okay.

I put my arm around her shoulders, walking us through the garage. "It's okay. You name it and it's yours."

She leans her head against my shoulder, way too proud to admit how tired she is, and gives me her sweet puppy dog eyes.

"Which candy?" I ask.

She laughs. "Reese's Peanut Butter Cups."

"Done."

We walk back inside the house—it was Timothy and

Elizabeth Bailey's house first—my parents. We've renovated from top to bottom, with the exception of a few bedrooms. Myles is at the door and Daisy lays in her bed.

When he tries to jump on Holly, I say, "Get down, Myles. How will we keep him away from the baby?"

She pets him and nuzzles her nose against his. "He'll be gentle."

"Gentle as a hyper elephant."

"No. You'll be good to the baby, right, Myles?" She scratches behind his ear, his favorite spot. She pets Daisy, whose body goes limp and falls deeper into her bed.

Holly walks to the couch and picks up the baby name book again.

I hate that damn thing.

"I'm going to search again, because pretty soon she's going to be born and we're going to be those parents holding Baby Bailey."

I shrug. "I don't think that's so bad. Her name is important." The last thing Holly needs is to be stressed out about the name of our baby.

"I don't want to introduce her to everyone like that." She rubs her belly with her free hand, staring down as if the baby is going to whisper what she wants to be named. "The least I can do for my first motherly duty is name my child."

The edge in her tone says now is not the time to argue this point. It's taken many a breakdown over the past months for me to figure that one out. "How about a hot bath before the ice cream dinner? I'll come up and we'll talk names?"

She smiles and sighs. "That sounds amazing."

I give her a kiss on the temple and a pat on the stomach before walking up the stairs to draw her bath.

While she soaks, I figure I'll lay in bed and catch some of

the spring training games, but the room to my right pulls me in.

The room screams girl. Four pale pink walls, a white crib with light yellow bedding. The spot above her crib is blank until we name her. The new changing table and dresser we bought two weeks ago are white as well. I never really cared what we had, especially after we tried for so long. And I too fear that this might be our only baby. I know Holly wants our daughter to have siblings because she didn't have any. Growing up with eight siblings might've been a pain in my ass sometimes, but I wouldn't change a thing.

The doctors say this pregnancy could restart her system. They've seen cases where people have gotten pregnant after rounds of IVF. But nothing is guaranteed.

The room looks like a unicorn threw up in it. As if she's coming out of the womb wearing a tutu and hair bows. I'm not sure how great of a girl dad I'll be, but one thing's for certain. She'll know how to throw a killer fastball.

2

Wyatt

"I'm doing it, aren't I?" I ask, ignoring Brooklyn's eyes on the back of my head, probably plotting my death.

I've read that sometimes a woman's personality changes when she's pregnant, and that's definitely been the case in our home. My sweet bride has turned to that thing from the *Alien* movie. She critiques everything and went so far as to tell me I don't love my child if I don't paint his room myself.

At first I thought she was pissed off because we were having a boy. One look at Brooklyn and everyone knows she's a girl mom. She's meant to shower our child with pretty clothes and cute hairstyles, take her shopping for prom dresses and enjoy spa trips together.

She's not the get-down-and-dirty type. What's going to happen when our boy brings her his first worm or outside creature? I'm determined that my son will not experience my upbringing of concrete parks in the middle of a city. My son will explore the outdoors. We'll do it together.

"That gray isn't the one I gave you. Did you give the right number to Jack?"

I clench my jaw. "Jack said he matched it."

"It doesn't look the same. It's lighter."

"Maybe you should call him."

"Don't get snippy with me. I'm just saying the gray was darker."

I push the roller up and down the wall, trying to have a light touch and feeling incompetent. I didn't paint the rest of my house because I suck at painting. I'm a firm believer everyone has their talents, and painting isn't one of mine. But here I am so that Brooklyn doesn't go into early labor from being angry that I hired professionals to decorate our nursery.

"This should've been done weeks ago."

I drop the roller, sit on the floor, and face her. "I'm about to go on strike."

Her angry stance loosens. "I know, okay? I'm cranky today." She stands with her hands on her hips, jutting out her very pregnant stomach.

She's cranky every day, but I don't say that.

"Do you think this is how I'm gonna be permanently now?" The hiccup in her voice makes me stand.

God, I hope not. I take her in my arms as close as we can get. She's beautiful pregnant, but I miss cradling her in my arms. "No. I think your hormones are on overload right now."

She hiccups a sob. "What if it's, like, me now? I mean, I'm going to nurse and all the same hormones..."

I kiss the top of her head. "You're going to be fine."

After a few minutes, her body shifts away from me and

her eyes examine the room. "Thank you for painting and not hiring someone."

I stare at all the edging I still have to do, not to mention some sticker thing she ordered online that I have to apply to the wall after it dries. Elephants and stars and moons is the theme she picked. Let's be honest, the kid is going to grow out of this within a year and I'm probably going to have to paint and decorate again to prove my love. By the time he's in college, I could probably get a side job as a painter.

"You're welcome." I smile at my wife.

"Oh, and don't forget the crib. Also, Holly said Austin already put in their car seats. We need to do that too. My mom went into labor early with Kingston and Juno, so we don't want to take any chances. They say you take after your mother usually. I will not be those parents who don't have the car seat in."

A drop of sweat drips down my back as my anxiety grows. "It will all be finished in time."

I have my doubts though. Maybe she wishes she married someone like her brothers because I've watched more how-to YouTube videos during her last trimester than I care to admit and I'm starting to feel as though I'm not a real man.

"You're the best." She kisses my cheek. "I'll go make you some lunch."

She leaves the room and I take the opportunity to sit down and look at the shit job I've done. The streak marks that some guy on YouTube told me was because I pushed too hard on the roller and apparently the only solution is to sand it down and repaint. No, thank you.

I have an entire hotel to run.

All the fears that keep me up at night resurface. Will I be enough for my son? My father and I had a strained relationship. His need for success was always more important than his need to be a present father. I swore from the moment Brooklyn told me she was pregnant that I would never be that man, but how much do genetics play into it? I'm at Glacier Point too much lately, doing what I promised I wouldn't—micromanaging my staff.

Brooklyn insists that I need to make this nursery for our son in order for it to be special, and maybe she's right. I pick up the paint roller and paint again just to get out of my own head—until a huge crash from downstairs causes me to stop mid-stroke and run.

3

———

Liam

Savannah's at the head of the conference table when I arrive at Bailey Timber near the end of the workday.

"Liam." Grandma Dori's there too and she crooks her finger, so I bend down and she kisses and hugs me. "This pregnancy has made her so nice," she remarks, patting my arm.

I say nothing because Savannah's within earshot. She's worried that pregnancy has made her soft, because she cries at commercials now.

"Let's keep her pregnant," Grandma Dori jokes.

I wouldn't mind Savannah being pregnant again. She'd take that pen that's in her hand and stab me in the throat if she heard me say that though, which is why I'm quietly waiting for her to finish talking to the company lawyer. Her distraction lets me eat her up like I used to, catalog all her features. I've begged and pleaded with her to let me paint her, but she keeps putting it off because she feels as though she's ugly now.

She's sexy as hell and it's not that her skin glows or her tits are fuller and bigger. It's the fact that she's growing *our* baby. A piece of her and me together is inside her. I never thought the moment would come where I would stand witness to this.

Sex has been a challenge as her stomach got bigger. She wasn't pleased this morning when she found out she could no longer look down and see her toes. Which is why I decided to surprise her today.

"Hey, Liam, good to see you." Dan puts his hand out and I shake it. "Any day now, huh?"

"Bite your tongue, Dan, we have three more weeks," Savannah says.

I love the fact that she says we.

Dan laughs and closes the door behind him, which is my signal to swivel my chair around and meet my wife at the end of the table.

My lips hit her cheek, and she leads my hand to her belly. "She's been kicking all day."

It's hard to explain how happy I am when I feel our baby move. I never really thought about what it would be like to have a baby of my own. I guess I always thought about after the baby was born, never what it would be like during the nine months of pregnancy. I'd have my hand permanently affixed to Savannah's stomach if she'd allow me, which we all know she won't.

I bend down and whisper, "Hey, sweet girl."

The baby's kicking subdues a bit.

"She just wanted her daddy."

Savannah smiles at me. "So did her mommy. Ready for dinner?"

"I assume you are?"

She laughs. "I'm starving."

"Did you eat lunch?" I ask.

She rolls her eyes, but it's been a hard lesson for her to learn that she needs to take time away from working to nourish the baby. She gets tunnel vision and doesn't come up for air. "Yes, Dad."

I fiddle with the tie of her dress. "Would you be mad if I untied this?"

"I would if you did it here."

I pull the tie a little and she shoots me her sternest look, but it's sweet compared to how she used to look at me before we got together. "Model for me?"

She pulls away from me. "I told you, no. I'm bloated and have gained so much weight because I eat the entire grocery store aisle of potato chips daily. She couldn't have cravings for sweets, it had to be salty."

I laugh because I just bought five bags of salt and vinegar chips at the store. Savannah will be done with them by week's end.

"Maybe she's a little like her mom—salty." I shrug.

"I hope she's a little sweet like her daddy too."

"Dinner?" I ask.

"Yeah, I need some grease and salt. Force me to have carrots tomorrow, okay?" She opens the door to the conference room.

"Sure," I say, following her.

Walking to her office, we run into Grandma Dori again, where she's bent over Savannah's new assistant's desk with a fist full of money.

"No, no. I have Brooklyn first, Savannah, and then Holly. Brooklyn is in such a sour mood lately, she needs to get that baby out of her."

"Grandma?" Savannah asks as though she has no idea what her grandma is doing.

I laugh behind her and that sweet Savannah from the conference room disappears. She glares at me over her shoulder.

"Are you betting on when we'll all deliver?"

Grandma Dori looks over her granddaughter's shoulder to me and smiles. "That I am." She turns back to Dedra. "You got that, right?"

Dedra bites her lip, looking at Savannah.

We all wait for the explosion. Each of us but Grandma Dori—she doesn't care.

Then Savannah holds her hand out toward me. "I'm definitely delivering first. I say me, Brooklyn, then Holly."

There's the competitive wife I know and love.

I pass her some money from my wallet.

"We've got one thing in common. Holly is last," Grandma Dori says.

Dedra smiles, her relief obvious. "Would you like to bet on times or days or pounds?"

Savannah sits down. "Seriously? Does no one work around here?" She surprises us all when she puts her hand out for more money and bets that our little girl's birth weight will be precisely seven pounds three ounces.

I help her stand afterward and she waddles into her office. Don't get me wrong, I love it. Her waddle is cute.

Dori leans in close. "See? Get her pregnant again right away. She's a delight."

I shake my head. "I'll do what I can."

Of course our sex life hasn't been affected at all. If anything, she's horny all the time, I was exhausted during her second trimester.

"Let's go." Savannah comes out of her office with her

coat in her hands and purse hanging off her shoulder. No computer or work to bring home. These are the good nights.

I take her coat because she'll never wear it even though spring is late to come this year, and we head to dinner.

———

AFTER SAVANNAH EATS A GREASY BURGER, fries, and onion rings at Lard Have Mercy, we drive home. My sweet ride comes into view when I pull in, though it's covered by a cloth tarp.

Sav climbs out of my new truck with help from me holding her arm as she steps onto the running board I installed after I purchased it. I love my car, but the seat belts in the back weren't safe enough for a baby. It's stored away for date nights and when our daughter is old enough.

She points at the empty car seat boxes by the trash can. "You already installed them?"

"In your car and the truck," I say.

She laughs as we walk into the house. "I didn't even notice when I got in. From what I hear, Austin had a horrible time with theirs."

"Why didn't he call me?" I unlock the door, but she takes my hand, leading me around the side of the house.

"Every man wants to install his own baby car seat."

She's right. I wouldn't allow anyone else to do that job. Her hand grows tighter around mine and I shiver from the cool breeze. Meanwhile, she walks around with only her wrap dress on as though it's eighty degrees out.

We get to the barn and she leans against the wood siding, waiting for me to get my keys out.

"What are we doing out here?" I ask.

She pushes off the wood and puts her arms around me,

kissing my jaw. "I want you to paint me. But be flattering. Don't go making it super realistic with my cankles and big butt."

I open up the barn and lead her in before shutting the door and locking it back up. "I wish you saw yourself through my eyes. You're the most incredibly sexy woman." I kiss her neck, my fingers fiddling with the tie of her dress.

"You have to say that. It's your baby I'm growing inside me."

"Nah, do you think I'd want to paint you if you were hideous?" I chuckle.

She smacks my shoulder and I chuckle in her ear, my tongue sliding around her earlobe as I unbutton the flap of the dress and it falls open, bearing her naked stomach to me.

I fall to my knees, cradle her belly in my hands, and press a light kiss to it. "You're beautiful."

Her smile says she believes me. I unhook her bra, letting it fall between us. After leading her to the couch, I strip off my shirt and get the canvas ready.

"How long will this take?" she asks.

"An hour maybe." I set up my paintbrushes. "Why?"

"Because staring at you with your shirt off and that fresh tattoo of my name on your skin is making me want to do something else on this couch." Her tongue slides out to wet her lip.

I drop the paintbrush and head over to my wife.

I can paint her tomorrow. After all, a happy wife means a happy life.

4

———

Unknown Female

I sit on the floor of my bathroom and tell Siri to set the timer for three minutes. Gnawing at my fingers, I try to block out all the negatives and only think of the positives. Is there ever really a perfect time to have a baby? No.

The fact that I've locked myself in my bathroom instead of involving him says I'm not sure how he'll handle the news. I mean, he can't be surprised if I am pregnant, right? If you have unprotected sex, there's obviously a chance this could happen.

My hand falls to my stomach as I wonder if—and slightly hope—there's a little one in there, regardless of what anyone outside this bathroom thinks.

The buzzer on my phone goes off. I inhale a deep breath before I pick the test up off the counter's edge. Bringing it down to me, I read the results and smile, releasing a relieved breath.

5

———

Sedona

"The party store is out of blue balloons. How does that happen?" I ask, dropping the bags filled with a million pink balloons. No blue.

"Without them, we're not representing Brooklyn," Juno says.

"Someone call Wyatt, he'll have them flown in," Phoenix jokes while she and Maverick straighten a tablecloth on the folding table.

When you decide to have a triple baby shower, there's only one place in town that can hold that many people. Thankfully, Cleo and Denver have an airplane hangar.

"Oh wait, I'll call Kingston. He's in Anchorage." I step out of the hangar and pull out my phone.

Before I have his name on the screen, I hear Phoenix sucking in helium and talking to Maverick. I swear, sometimes I wonder how it's possible we're twins.

There are three missed calls from Jamison that I ignored last night after I flew in. The red notification circle feels like a blinking red light wanting me to give it the attention it needs. Later, I tell myself, and I dial Kingston.

"You back in Lake Starlight?" he answers.

I laugh at my brother's ability to never bother with semantics like greetings. "I am."

"Awesome. I'm just pulling out of the station now. I gotta change. This is casual, right?"

"Before you head back here, can you stop at a party store in Anchorage and grab some blue balloons? They didn't have any at the one in town."

"Sure."

"Great, thanks."

"Wait, what's up with Jamison?"

Kingston never asks me personal questions. Mostly because he never wants me to pry into his affairs. The fact that he's still pining away for Stella is supposed to be top secret, but we all know it. At least Phoenix, Juno, and I do. He liked one of Stella's posts on Instagram the other day, so we know he follows her. Which cannot be good.

"Why?" I clear my throat. "I mean, what do you mean?"

"The guys and I were watching ESPN last night. One of the guys at the station, Lou, he's really into soccer and noticed Jamison wasn't playing. He didn't get traded, did he?"

No. "No. He hurt his ankle during the last game."

"Oh, I swear I didn't see him on the bench either."

Okay, Kingston, I get the point. "Well, you know how they only have the cameras at certain angles. He was there."

After a minute, Kingston says, "I'm glad he wasn't traded. I know the long distance between the two of you before was hard. Okay, I'm almost at the party store. Anything else?"

I step back into the hangar. "Do we need anything else from the party store in Anchorage?"

Phoenix inhales helium. "More helium?" Then she giggles and Maverick laughs at his one-day stepmom.

"Think we're good," I say.

"Tell Phoenix to save some for the rest of us. I'll drop off the balloons before I change."

"Cool, thanks, King," I say. We hang up, and I throw my phone into my purse before digging out the baby confetti to put on each table. "Kingston's gonna grab some blue balloons."

"Good," Juno says from her task of arranging the dessert table. "I'm just getting the table ready for Greta."

"Is she bringing any donuts or cookies?" Maverick asks from across the room where he and Phoenix are now putting photo picture props by the rented photo booth.

"Who's in charge of games again?" I ask.

"Me!" Denver walks in with metal keg bins.

"This isn't a keg party," Juno says, her voice missing its usual niceness.

Cleo walks in right after him with pieces of paper in hand.

"What games do you have planned?" I ask.

Denver winks and clicks his tongue on the roof of his mouth as though he's just waiting until we hear how awesome they are.

"We've got... open door number one, Cleo..." He gives his best Bob Barker impersonation.

Cleo rolls her eyes. "I'm not a part of this." She drops the papers on the table and walks over to us.

"Babe!" Denver drops the bins and takes the tape and large poster board, positioning it on the wall.

"Denver!" Phoenix scolds, her hand covering Maverick's eyes.

I'm fairly sure Juno and I close our eyes and open them slowly. Sure enough, it's a print-out of a giant vulva.

"Phoenix," Maverick whines and attempts to pry her fingers off his eyes.

"Get it off the wall," Phoenix bites out, plastering Maverick's back to her chest, one of her hands over his eyes and the other across his stomach.

"I told you it was inappropriate," Cleo singsongs and disappears back out the door.

"What on Earth?" Juno asks.

Seeing that Denver has no plans of taking it down, Phoenix steps forward with Maverick, his eyes still covered until they're by the doors. "Head into the office while I have a conversation with Uncle Denver."

When the door shuts behind Maverick, Phoenix swats Denver with both hands. "What were you thinking?"

Denver dodges and weaves out of the way. "Come on. It's Pin the Sperm on the Vulva."

Yep, of course, the small pieces of papers Cleo was holding are cut-out sperm.

"How much time did you spend on this?" Juno asks.

"I was up until two cutting out the sperms."

I pick up one. "You glued googley eyes on them?"

Denver smiles proudly. "Of course."

The rest of us sit there and stare at him as we have most of our life—baffled at how he's biologically related to us.

"I'm thinking the game could go in the storage room or something," I suggest before Phoenix loses her shit. Although stepmomhood has calmed her wild ways, she still has low patience when it comes to Denver's antics.

"Fine. But it was going to be the highlight of the night."

Denver takes the tape off the wall, and Juno helps him carry the sperm.

Phoenix sits down at the table. "Are we really going to ask people if they want to go into a closet to play a game?"

"Want me to go get Maverick?"

She waves. "Nah, I'm sure he's playing some game on Denver's computer. The kid knows his password since Maverick had to fix something for him the other day."

I sit next to her. "You look tired."

"I am. My schedule is grueling but totally worth it. Next month we'll just be working on the album, so it will be calmer." She straightens her back. "Enough about me. You've been tight-lipped since you arrived." She narrows her eyes at me.

That's the thing about being a twin. She already knows something's up. I knew when things weren't going well with her in LA before she came home.

"Nothing. I worry about Juno though."

Phoenix leans back in her chair, crosses her arms, and raises her eyebrows at me.

"I might stay home for a little while. Help out with all the babies."

Her expression doesn't change.

My lip trembles because I can't fool my twin.

I press my lips together, but she sees it and her hand covers mine. "What happened, Sedona?"

I scan the room. It's so pretty for my sisters' and Holly's baby shower. I am not going to ruin it with my own drama. "Can we talk about it later?"

"Come over tonight. Spend the night at my place?"

I've been staying with Juno since Kingston was on shift and they're both single, but I need Phoenix's advice. "Yeah, okay."

She squeezes my hand and pulls me into a chair hug. "Am I going to want to fly to New York City and knee him in the balls?"

"You'd have to go to Scotland."

She pulls back from our embrace, looking worried, and my nose tickles from the rush of tears that want to spill. The best thing about Phoenix is she knows me better than anyone. That thought alone has scared me since she got with Griffin. Do I know her the best out of everyone still? There are probably things she shares with Griffin that I have no idea about.

"Bobbing for Nipples?" Juno asks Denver as they walk out of the storage locker. "Where did you find these games? What happened to eating a jar of baby food and guessing how many candies are in a baby bottle?"

Phoenix is quick to let me go because if she gives them the idea that there's something wrong, then pretty soon, Grandma Dori will end up on my ass about it.

Calista runs into the hangar with Dion right on her heels and Phoebe waddling after. All three are pushing strollers with baby dolls inside. Harley follows, her skin looking pasty and her hair thrown into a bun. She's wearing yoga pants and a torn sweatshirt.

"Why do you need all these strollers and babies, Denver?" Harley asks.

All of us turn our heads in his direction, but his mischievous smile says it all.

6

———

Kingston

I open the door of the party supply place for a mom and her daughter with a huge bunch of pink and silver balloons. Inside the store is a line of twenty people waiting for one lonely sales associate who looks like a high schooler.

Scanning the aisle signs, I search for balloons. I'm sure I can flirt my way to the front of the line if all I have is a bag of blue balloons.

"Bailey," a guy calls as I walk by one aisle.

I step back, assuming it's a guy from the station.

Unfortunately, it's not a guy from the station.

"Owen," I say.

"Don't sound too excited." He puts his arm around the girl he's with.

He's delusional to think I want everything of his. I only wanted one thing of his, my entire life.

"I just got off shift."

"You're a firefighter?" the girl asks, her eyes focusing on my jacket.

I could say yeah and excuse myself from this conversation. That would be the right thing to do. Call me immature after this stunt, but my history with Owen is long. "Smokejumper during the summer. Firefighter during winter."

Her gaze soaks me in again, except this time her body shifts away from Owen.

"And you get paid shit money for putting your life on the line," Owen says.

"At least I don't smell like fish every day."

"You're on call twenty-four seven during the summer. Talk about sucking."

"You're on a boat with a bunch of dudes for months at a time." I raise my eyebrows.

He opens his mouth and shuts it. I'm not naïve enough to think he won't come up with something. When all else fails, he'll go for the jugular.

"Are you guys friends, or not?" The girl laughs awkwardly.

Does this girl think we're competing for her or something? She's wrong. The girl we're still competing over has moved on without a glance back at either of us.

"We are. Kingston's just pissed because I dated the girl he wanted all through high school. Slow healing wound, I guess." Owen's smug look should be stripped away by my fist.

"What are you doing at a party store?" I ask, purposely ignoring his jab so it looks as though that wound has healed. It hasn't, but there's a lot Owen doesn't know. Things I'll never tell him.

"My sister's having a baby!" the girl exclaims. "I'm

throwing her a shower. And Owen came to help carry the bags."

I pat him on the shoulder. "He's good for that. Using his muscles instead of his brain."

My dig at Owen's intelligence breezes by the girl but not Owen, who scowls.

"Aren't, like, all your sisters pregnant?" he asks.

"Jealous?"

He always loved coming to my house because of my sisters. If I wanted to be a real jerk, I could talk about Phoenix being a pop star and Griffin, who's a popular music producer. The girl would probably abandon Owen and run into my arms, but she's not the girl I want.

"Poor Liam, Savannah has to be a bear pregnant."

I shrug. The girl turns to peruse some items on the shelf, and I snag three bags of blue balloons. "Actually, she's pretty low-key. Everyone's betting on how soon Liam knocks her up again to keep her that way."

Owen laughs. "She's scary."

I nod a few times and he rocks back on his heels. I lift the bags of balloons. "I'm on balloon duty for their shower, so I should go before one of them calls."

"Cool." He shakes my hand.

"Nice meeting you," I say to the girl.

She turns, and her eyes zoom in on my jacket again. "You t—you're a Bailey? Like from Bailey Timber?"

Owen groans. He's always hated that people in our family are held in high regard. I asked him once when his jealousy was at peak level if he'd rather have his parents die for the exchange. He shut up pretty quick.

"I am," I say.

"Oh. My friend just started working there."

"Awesome." I back-step down the aisle, wanting to get away from this conversation.

"She was telling me the sad story about your parents. I'm sorry."

I shrug as if I don't care that my parents died. "It was, like, fifteen years ago."

Then I do the math in my head. It *will* be fifteen years ago this year. Fuck, Grandma D is definitely going to want to do something big to honor their memory.

"That long? You were young when it happened."

"I was—"

Owen beats me to it. "He was ten."

The memory of hiding in his treehouse fills my head. I couldn't stand to be at my house during those weeks immediately after the accident. The funeral preparations, Austin returning home, Rome and Denver moments away from winding up in jail from all the stupid shit they were pulling.

I smile at Owen, and he smiles back. He's probably remembering the same things I am.

The secret meals he brought me when his parents watched television after dinner. The sleeping bag and the fact that he slept out there with me even though he was scared to death of spiders. The traps we made for when Austin came to take me home. Even him kicking Austin in the shin when Austin successfully carried me out of the treehouse.

"Go. Maybe we'll grab a beer next week or something." Owen nods toward the end of the aisle.

"Yeah. Okay. Good seeing you."

"You too."

I head to the checkout, thankful the line is much shorter than when I arrived. Hearing Phoenix sucking the helium out of the tank, I figured she won't be the only one, so I opt to have them all blown up.

While I wait, I pull out my phone, scanning through Instagram posts until my thumb pauses on one of Stella.

She's still beautiful. She was at a race for Lupus, the picture of her crossing the finish line of a 5k. Which is huge for her since she hated all exercise when she was younger.

Her smile is contagious, and I smile involuntarily at seeing her happy. It's a stark difference from when she's around me. When she sees me, the past comes back and reminds her of what transpired between us. A time she'd like to forget, which sucks for me.

I click the heart button but don't comment. After shutting off my phone, I pocket it and grab the balloons to celebrate my family's happily ever afters. One day I need to move on and stop comparing all women to Stella, but today isn't that day.

7

———

Rome

I pull the truck to a stop in front of the hangar and see that Harley's minivan is already parked.

"She's not supposed to be here," I tell Colin.

We climb out of the truck, and he opens the back doors to unload all the food we prepared.

"Dada!" Phoebe spots me first and walks out of the hangar, but Dion runs faster and makes Phoebe lose her footing, falling onto the gravel parking lot.

"Dion," I sigh.

The boy never knows who's around him or what he's destroying. I catch him in my arms and walk us over to Phoebe, who's now on her bum, crying.

I place Dion down on the gravel. "You have to keep an eye out for your little sister."

Dion nods and throws a football to Maverick, who's also out front.

"Hey, Maverick," I say, picking up Phoebe.

Her small arms wrap tightly around my neck. I'll never grow tired of this stage. The one where she thinks her daddy is her savior. Calista is like a six-year-old turning sixteen lately. I see her gravitating toward Harley, intrigued by her makeup and playing dress-up.

"Hey, Uncle Rome." Maverick tosses the football back to Dion without any gusto. Sports just aren't the kid's thing.

"Don't forget, Dion, you have to do something Maverick wants to do too," I say.

Dion nods, but it's never gonna happen.

"You okay, sweet girl?" I run my hand down Phoebe's back while I enter the hangar.

She wiggles to get free when she spots her uncle Denver filling buckets with water. "Wawa," she yells and runs to Denver.

"Ladies." I bow to three of my sisters, Harley, and Cleo when I find them all sitting at a table. "I see the set-up has stalled."

"We're waiting for the blue balloons from Kingston," Juno sneers.

The woman's mood lately is like a cat's. One minute she's all loving and sweet, and the next she's hissing and swatting with her paws.

I find my way over to Harley. She looks rundown, but I'm not gonna say anything. The other morning, she bit my head off when I asked her to pass the pepper.

"Hey babe," I say, kissing her cheek.

"Hey."

Yeah, I think I'll just bring in the food.

"Cleo, where did they deliver the fridge?" I had a fridge delivered here for the party because I won't have people get sick from spoiled food.

Cleo is staring at Denver pretending to dunk Phoebe in the water. My daughter giggles uncontrollably every time he lowers her closer.

"Cleo?" I ask again.

She glances at me but seems to have no idea what I asked.

"The refrigerator?"

She smiles and nods, standing. "We had them put it by the storage locker."

She leads me to the other side of the hangar, her eyes continuing to stray toward Denver and Phoebe interacting. Maybe someone has baby fever. God knows Denver will think of it as a competition whenever they do get married and start trying.

Colin walks in with the trays of food.

"You've done amazing." Harley snags a Caprese kabob off the tray and eats it, grabbing one more before Colin can get away.

"Hungry?" I ask, chuckling.

"No time to eat," she mumbles around a mouthful of food.

I slide my arm around Harley's back and pull her to me. "Tomorrow I've got the kids, so you can sleep in."

It's been crazy with the restaurant. We're opening a second location in Anchorage, which has meant me traveling every day. Once it's open, it will be worth it. I'll lose Colin at the Lake Starlight location so he can be the head chef in Anchorage, but it's all part of the plan to secure the future I want for my family.

"Look!" Calista interrupts us.

I look down to see that my daughter has stuffed a balloon up her shirt. Harley laughs and I knock the balloon out of her belly.

"Dad!" she whines. Lately she's mixed the dad and the daddy. I fucking hate it, but Harley tells me it's all part of her growing older. I still hate it.

"You've seen your mom pregnant. It's not fun, is it?" I look at Harley, whose smile drops. Not like she's pissed off at me or anything, but she's not happy either. "Ask your aunts today how great they feel. They can't even see their swollen ankles."

Harley grips my arm so hard, I have no choice but to tear my arm out of her grasp. She stares at me as if she's telepathically telling me how to handle this situation and I'm doing a piss-poor job.

What am I supposed to say? Pregnancy is fucking fantastic. Just count down the days until you too can carry a baby in your tummy? Fuck no. This is my daughter. Then my mind descends into thoughts of how she would get pregnant, which means she has to—

I rub my temples. "God help me, the next one better be a boy."

Calista picks up the balloon, puts it back under her shirt, and holds one hand to her back, extending her stomach, and waddles over to her aunts, who all laugh.

"We're having more?" Harley asks.

I shrug, not really sure. We haven't talked about it, but then again, we didn't talk about it with Dion or Phoebe or Calista.

"Last week you were talking about getting the big V," she reminds me.

That's because our house was all screams and tantrums like our children had been possessed. All I wanted was some Sunday morning sex with my wife and Dion was banging on the door because Calista had changed the television channel, which woke up Phoebe.

I shrug. "I was pissed."

"And now?"

"Do you really think I should have a procedure that would permanently stop us from having more? Wasn't it just six months ago when my sisters announced their pregnancies that we were having sex like crazy so you could be pregnant with them?" I laugh.

The one and only time we couldn't get pregnant was when we were actually trying.

"Yeah, but Sunday morning sex isn't going to happen all that often if we keep having babies. Birth control doesn't work for us. Maybe we need to talk about what we want."

Her face is serious with no hint of a smile. I know she's been tired and frustrated lately, what with not being able to take on as many massage clients as she wants.

I slide my arms behind her back and pull her toward me. "Okay, we'll talk about it tomorrow."

"Okay," she says.

There's something off with her. I think it's time for a date night.

8

___

Denver

After I set up all the games, I go back to my office, open up the last drawer on the right, and dig behind a pile of papers I know Cleo would never go through. It's safer than the house for sure. She can be nosy.

The diamond sparkles under the fluorescent light. I've thought of a million ways to ask her to marry me. Take her up into the mountains, back to the first place we stayed overnight together. I could drop to a knee in the middle of the ice cave. Or when we're alone in a tent where no witnesses can capture our most precious moment.

None of it seems right. None of it fits *us*.

The door from the outside opens and I slam the box shut and drop it into the bottom drawer.

Cleo walks into the office. She hasn't been herself all day. She's done what's been asked of her in regard to hanging streamers and opening the tables and chairs we rented. But she has no enthusiasm for it.

"Come sit on daddy's lap." I slide out my chair and pat my leg.

She rolls her eyes. See what I mean? Back in the day, she would have just scolded me, but she would've come over.

"Come on."

She slowly walks over to me, and when she gets closer, I capture her so she falls into my lap.

"Talk to me." I move her hair off her neck, kissing her.

Her back sinks into my chest. "It's just all the changes. Three babies at once."

"Are you sure there's nothing else?" She squirms to get away, but I hold her firm around her stomach. "It's me. You can tell me anything."

She's silent.

"Cleo?"

"I have to go help with the shower. I just came in to get my phone."

"Babe?"

She wiggles and I release her, so she goes to stand at her desk across from me.

"Okay, fine. I can take a hint. Maybe you can talk to one of my sisters then."

She says nothing, fiddling with her phone.

Nothing grates on me more than silence and Cleo knows this. If she doesn't tell me, I can't fix it, and I don't want to celebrate tonight with her being grumpy.

"Just tell me!" My voice comes out louder than intended.

She looks up at me from the phone as a tear slips from her eye.

I stand and walk around to her side of the desk, taking her in my arms. "Why are you crying? What's the matter?"

She sobs into my chest and I soothe her as much as I can without knowing why she's crying in the first place.

"You have to tell me now."

She shakes her head. "It's embarrassing."

"Nothing should be embarrassing with me. I wore a bright green Speedo that my dick didn't fit into in front of you. Remember that?"

She laughs.

"How about the time I forgot the flint when we went on that excursion and it took me two hours to start a fire with two sticks? That was aired on national television and I'm supposed to be a professional survivalist."

Her laugh increases.

I place my forefinger under her chin, forcing her to look at me. Her eyes are red and swollen from the short stint of tears. She shakes her head.

"I don't care what it is. Just tell me."

Her forehead falls onto my chest and her arms lay limp at her sides. "I feel like we're stalled," she mumbles, but I catch it.

"Stalled?" I sit on the edge of her desk and hold her out in front of me so I can see her.

She shifts her weight from side to side, staring at her feet.

"What do you mean stalled?"

"Like everyone's life is moving forward and here we are."

"The business is great. We booked more clients this year than the previous ten. The show is starting its third season and they're talking about renewing us for another three."

She nods. "I know business is great." She peeks up at me through her eyelashes.

I'm always a little slow on the uptake. Damn it. She's questioning my commitment. I knew I'd waited too long to propose. I didn't want to scare her off by doing it too early and now I've done the opposite. Of course she's upset.

"Are you saying you want more?" I ask.

She chews on the inside of her lip and peeks up again. She shrugs.

"Cleo?"

"This is so embarrassing. And now you're going to propose just to keep me even though you don't want to marry me. We'll get married and have kids and in five or ten years, whenever that itch comes, you'll wake up and realize I pressured you into marrying me..."

She rambles on, and I allow her to because her pacing allows me to walk over to my desk and open up the drawer.

I wanted to make this magical, special, a story she'd tell our children. Me in a suit on bended knee in the middle of some garden, the ring box open as she walked in wearing a dress that I'd bought and had delivered to her. But that's not us. We were business partners before we were best friends and best friends before we were lovers.

She's my confidant and the only one I want standing by my side. This business is what brought us together in the first place, so why shouldn't it be now?

"Cleo," I say to stop her, dropping down on bended knee.

She catches a glimpse of me from the corner of her eye. "Get up!"

I chuckle. "No."

"Yes. Get up! You are not proposing to me after I just rambled on like some lunatic. I know we have it good, I do."

I don't get up. "Cleo Dawson?"

She breaks the distance and tries to pull me up by my arms. "Don't do it, Denver. Not now. Don't!"

I can't stop laughing at her. "Will you—"

Her hand lands over my mouth. "Nope. Don't say it."

"Will you marry me," I mumble under her hand.

Her hand drops as she falls to the floor in front of me. "Denver…"

I take her left hand. "I'm not doing this because of what you said. I'm doing this because I've tried to plan the perfect time to propose but this is it. It should be here, where it all began. I love you, Cleo Dawson, and I want you to be by my side for the rest of our lives. It dawned on me just now that I can't give you the perfect proposal because our life is going to be far from perfect. We're going to fight, and if you're still with me in fifty years, I'll be just as surprised as you."

"But—"

I place my finger in front of her lips. "It's impolite to talk during your proposal."

She giggles. Thank God. I'm not bombing at this.

"You're it for me. You're the lucky lady who gets to be Mrs. Denver Bailey."

She knocks her shoulder with mine and shakes her head.

"I meant I'm the lucky bastard who gets to be Mr. Cleo Dawson Bailey." She smiles, and I say, "But you have to say yes first."

She puts her hands on my cheeks, staring into my eyes as though there's a truth there. "How long have you had that ring?"

"About six months."

"You really want to do this?" she whispers.

"Since when do you know me to do something I don't want to do?" I take the ring out of the box and bring her left hand between us. "Cleo Dawson, will you completely ruin your life and marry me?"

She laughs, and her forehead falls to mine. "Yes."

I slide the ring onto her finger. It's not nearly as big as I'd love her to have, but one day we'll upgrade. "I promise I'll give you a happy life."

"Denver?"

"Yeah?"

"Kiss me."

I lean in and kiss my future wife. Along with a few other things while the rest of my family is busy organizing the baby shower.

9

———

Juno

Kingston arrives late, but he's got all the blue balloons already blown up. What I'm more surprised to see is Selene from the Cozy Cottage Bed and Breakfast climbing down from his truck. I'd started to wonder if she was coming at all since most of the other townies have already arrived.

I meet him and grab a bundle of the balloons. "Hi, Selene."

"Juno, you look beautiful," she says.

"You too," I say.

She walks up the gravel walkway and through the hangar doors.

"Why are you bringing Selene to the party?"

Kingston is like the rest of my brothers—he'll never decline a favor someone asks of him. Which is wonderful, but if he's in communication with Selene, I worry that he could get sucked into all things Stella again. That would be about as good for him as if his hobby was snake charming.

"Her car wouldn't start, conked out. Found her on the side of the road," he says.

"Oh. And what did you talk about on the way over?"

He blows out an annoyed breath. "Give me a break, okay? We both kept Stella out of the conversation. Ever since Colton got engaged, you've been..."

He lets his words trail off, because he'd never say I'm being a bitch.

I am.

I'm fully aware of it. Since Kingston has lived with me for years, I wouldn't be completely offended if he did call me out on it. All of my family members are shying away from asking me anything about Colton and his future wife.

"I know, okay? But all you had to do was pick up some blue balloons. I had to plan this entire thing."

Kingston puts his arm around my shoulders. "Hey, do you want to talk?"

I shake my head. "Thanks, but it's done. There's nothing I can do to change it."

He stops me before walking into the hangar, nudging me off to the side. "Do you honestly think if you told Colton you feel more than friendship for him that he'd still marry her?"

I shrug.

"Juno, the man loves you. He's crazy about you, always has been. But you pushed him into the friend zone for so long."

"Exactly. I can't very well screw up his entire life now because I think I might like him more than a friend. What if it's only because he's taken?"

Kingston blows out a breath. He's annoyed. Probably because when Kingston sees something he wants, he goes for it. He doesn't let fear handicap him like I do. He almost tore his friendship with Owen apart to get Stella. I'm not built like him, and I don't think he understands why not.

"It isn't because he's taken." He says it like, *open your eyes, Juno.*

I shrug and frown. "It could be. We've been friends forever. Maybe I'm just afraid that our friendship will change now that he has someone in his life."

My brother shakes his head. "If you're not going to say anything, then I suggest you suck it up because he just pulled in with her."

My heart shrivels a bit and sinks to the depths of my stomach.

"I'll manage just fine," I say and detour into the hangar without looking back.

"What's up, Colt?" Kingston says behind me—purposely being loud, I imagine.

"Finally the blue ones." Sedona takes them from my hands. "Brooklyn has yet to arrive."

I hand them off and beeline it toward the bar. I'm going to need something to take the edge off and get through this baby shower.

Unfortunately, I run smack-dab into Grandma Dori.

"Juno."

"Grandma," I say, trying to weave around her.

She grabs my upper arms. "How are you? You've been so depressed these last few months. I told you I could help you at work. You don't even have to pay me."

"I'm good. I don't have a lot of clients right now anyway."

Truth is, my matchmaking business is dying a slow death. That's what happens when you stop believing in true love. Not that I'm in love with Colton. I'm definitely not. It's just a jealousy thing because he spends so much time with *her*.

"Then it's perfect."

My eyes zero in on the bar. I need a drink so badly. Something to numb this anxiety. "What's perfect?"

"Everyone always thinks young people need to find love, but the older generation needs love too. We're not dead yet."

My stomach clenches. "Grandma, are you telling me you want me to fix you up?"

She smacks my arm rather hard. "Juno Iris Bailey, I would never disrespect your grandfather like that."

"I wouldn't say it's disrespecting. You'd just be having a companion for—" I stop talking because from the look on her face, she might just haul off and smack me.

"Not me! Ethel and a few other ladies at game night. We were going to do a mixed game night, but it's hard to find men as you get older. They die too young."

I nod. "Are you expecting me to come to Northern Lights Retirement Home and do a rendition of *The Dating Game*?"

Her eyes light up. She's got to be kidding me.

"Perfect. Oh, they'd love it. I'll talk with Carolyn and we'll plan what night."

Carolyn is the events planner at Northern Lights. I'll need to get to her first so that her schedule is packed and she can't fit me in.

But for Grandma Dori, I nod. "Okay, then we can talk logistics."

"We went antiquing in Greywall the other day. Ethel saw a man doing that tai chi stuff. She was very enamored with him. Maybe you could find him and bring him along."

I stare at her for a moment. She's serious. Of course she is. "Sure thing. I'll go to Greywall and wait for some man to come to the park and do tai chi. Then I'll convince him to get in a car with me to play *The Dating Game* at a retirement community."

She scowls at my sarcasm. "You know, I love you, but I don't like you right now. I'm trying to help you." She walks away, mumbling to herself about me being her toughest case.

Whatever. The last thing I need is her getting even more involved in my life.

I mindlessly walk toward the bar until I look up to find Colton and Brigitte. She couldn't be more different than me physically. She's tall and rail-thin with long dark hair that's usually pulled into a ponytail. I'm short, curvy, and known around Lake Starlight as the adopted Bailey because I look like none of them. Truth is, I resemble Holly more than Austin.

"Juno!" Colton spots me before I can get lost in the crowd again.

I smack on my best smile, but Colton's lips dip into a frown. He knows me way too well.

"Hey," I say.

"Can I get you a drink?" Colton asks.

Brigitte turns around with the drink Colton must've already gotten her. "Juno," she says sweetly with her beautiful French accent. "So good to see you."

Brigitte places her hands on my shoulders and bends to kiss each of my cheeks. I go along with the dramatic hello.

"You too." I force a smile.

When the bartender hands Colton his beer, Colton stops the bartender from moving to the next customer. "I need a —" he stops and looks at me. "What's the drink today?"

Brigitte looks back and forth between us. It's not an inside joke. Everyone in my family knows I'm not a usual kind of girl when it comes to drinks.

"I'm really into flavored vodkas right now," I say.

Colton smiles, his perfectly white teeth practically glowing.

"Get her a strawberry lemonade. Strawberry vodka with lemonade. Three-fourths ratio vodka," a deep voice says before a large arm wraps around my shoulders.

Colton's nostrils flare.

I look to my side. "Trey Galger. What are you doing here?" I ask with a smile.

This is about to get even more uncomfortable. Quick.

"No hug?" Trey asks me.

My throat coats with dryness and I raise up on my tiptoes to hug him.

He swings me around before placing my feet back on the floor. "I'm here with Thorne, working on a new artist. Lucky you, we didn't get enough done, so I'm spending the night." He winks one of his sparkling blue eyes.

I ignore his innuendo. "Well, lucky you, you get to be at a baby shower. Yippee."

"Here you go, Juno." Colton sets my drink in front of me. "I'm Colton." He puts his hand out between us.

"Nice to meet you. I think I met you before." Trey bobs his head side to side as though he's trying to remember.

"And this is his fiancée, Brigitte. She's from Paris," I say.

Trey's eyes fall over her and I'm fairly sure he's actively trying to keep his jaw off the floor and the drool in his mouth. "Hey."

They shake hands too, but it's more Brigitte putting her hand in his, all dainty and feminine. We all stand in a small circle in silence. I tip my cup to my lips and gulp.

"Whoa, killer." Trey puts his hand on my drink.

"I was thirsty. I've been here all day. Which actually, I need to go check on... my sister."

I leave the group before anyone can object. Savannah is talking with Bailey Timber people, so I stop at Rome and Harley, who both look at me as though I'm interrupting their conversation.

Okay, I kind of am.

"Continue talking. I just needed to escape," I say.

Harley looks over my shoulder as her hand runs down my arm. God, I'm so sick of the pitying looks everyone is giving me these days.

I can tell by the way Rome is staring at me that I'm not welcome in their conversation, so I make an excuse about how I'm going to go check whether Brooklyn has arrived yet. I walk to the other side of the hangar and open the door to peek out in the parking lot, and lo and behold, Wyatt's pulling in. We're a half hour into this party, but at least now all the guests of honor have arrived. The sooner we start this thing, the sooner we can all go home.

Wyatt blows out a breath as he steps down from his fancy truck and rounds the front to open the door for Brooklyn.

I wait patiently as he helps her climb down. "Ridiculous. You have millions of dollars and I have to worry every time I climb in and out of your truck whether I'm going to fall forward and injure our baby."

Wyatt says nothing, but his hands clench at his sides.

"How's it going, you two?" I ask.

"Ugh, don't even ask," Brooklyn says, stopping and hugging me when she comes through the door. "It's beautiful. Thank you for organizing everything."

"I'm kind of hoping for early delivery," Wyatt whispers as he passes me. "Bar over there?" He points and sets off, a man on a mission.

I feel you, bro.

"Don't go getting drunk. If my water breaks, I don't need a drunk dad to take care of too," Brooklyn calls after him.

I cringe as heads turn. Wyatt raises his hand and keeps walking.

"So how's the pregnancy?" I ask.

"I know I'm being bitchy, okay?"

Looks like we're two peas in a pod, except I get to drink.

Thank God for that. I bring my cup to my mouth and toss back the rest of the contents. A few more of these and I should be good.

10

Calista

Mommy and Daddy are talking in the corner with no smiles. No smiles means it's something serious.

I ditch Grandma Dori and step closer.

"Why would you ever think..." Daddy says.

"I locked myself in the bathroom and..." Mommy's shoulders rise and fall. I can't hear her, so I lean toward them.

Then Daddy smiles. A big smile like when he comes home from work and we all run at him.

"Calista"—Dion grabs my sleeve—"Uncle Denver said we can play a game."

I shrug him off and push him away.

Daddy hugs Mommy then places his hand on her belly.

I know what that means.

"*No!*" I stomp over to them.

"Calista, what's wrong?" Mommy asks.

"No!" I repeat.

Daddy lowers down to my height. "Did something happen?"

"Why did you put your hand on Mommy's belly?" I ask, my hands on my hips.

Daddy looks up at Mommy. "I was just hugging Mommy."

"No. You put your hand on her stomach like you did when Phoebe was in there."

Daddy looks at Mommy. They both look around the room.

"It's a secret. Can you keep a secret?" he asks me.

I nod. It better be something other than another Phoebe in there. She cries too much.

Mommy bends down too, and they pull me into a circle. Only us three. My favorite always.

"You're going to be a big sister," Daddy says.

"I'm already a big sister," I say.

"Yes, but there's another baby in Mommy's stomach. You're going to be a big sister again," Daddy says.

I get really hot and my lips get kind of tight. "*A baby!*"

Daddy and Mommy's smiles disappear, and Daddy pulls me in tighter.

"Lower your voice," he says, using that mean voice.

"What was that, Calista?" Uncle Austin asks. He and Aunt Holly walk over.

"Mommy's having a baby. Again!" I yell and stomp my foot.

"Shut up?" Aunt Holly says. "Really?"

Why does she look happy? Doesn't she know this is awful?

Mommy's cheeks turn red. "Go figure. You're ready to pop and now I get pregnant. I'm destined to always be pregnant alone."

Aunt Holly laughs and hugs Mommy. I roll my eyes.

"Man, we'll never catch up," Uncle Austin says to Daddy, and they do something with their hands before hugging.

All the rest of our family comes over and hugs Mommy and Daddy, saying things to me like, "don't you love being a big sister" or "is there a three-peat big sister shirt."

I'm surrounded by a big circle of people and I cross my arms. "I don't want to be a big sister again."

Everyone looks at me, all laughing and smiling. Did they not hear me?

"Yeah, I get what she's saying," Uncle Austin says, patting me on the head.

"I never wanted Brooklyn," Aunt Savannah says.

Daddy raises his hand. "I wanted Kingston!"

"So did I," Uncle Denver says.

"A little brother to beat up on," they say together.

"Oh, you could have twins!" Aunt Phoenix says.

Mommy puts her hand on her stomach and smiles at Daddy. Like two babies would be a good thing. That would be the worst thing ever!

I stomp on Aunt Phoenix's foot.

"Ouch!" She looks down at me.

It's like the domino game Daddy tried to teach me, but Dion kept knocking it over. One by one, everyone looks at me and no one is smiling.

Daddy reaches into the circle and pulls me out of the middle.

"Don't be too hard on her, Rome, she's just speaking her mind. Nothing wrong with that," Aunt Phoenix yells, but Daddy's leading us out of the party to the outside.

Mommy follows us. When Daddy stops, he bends back down so his eyes can look at mine.

"Calista, why would you do that to Aunt Phoenix?" Mommy asks because Daddy keeps shaking his head.

"Who wants to bob for nipples?" Uncle Denver yells from inside.

Mommy and Daddy ignore him.

"I don't want to share," I mumble.

Mommy and Daddy look at one another again.

"I know it's hard being the oldest—" Daddy says.

"No, you don't. You aren't the oldest. I miss everything. Last week when we went to the zoo, I wanted to see the polar bears you promised after lunch, but then Phoebe whined and threw up and we left."

Daddy sits on the ground and puts me into his lap. "I'm sorry. You're right."

I lay my head on his shoulder and Mommy puts her fingers through my hair. She used to put it in curls with braids and ponytails. Now she tells me I'm big enough to brush it myself.

"How about we go to the zoo, just us three, next weekend?" Mommy says.

"Really?"

She nods. "We'll get a babysitter for Dion and Phoebe."

Daddy smiles at me. "Good?"

I nod.

"And me and Mommy will make sure to make time for all of you separately, but you can't stomp on someone's foot just because you didn't like what they said. You have to apologize to Aunt Phoenix."

"Okay." I frown. I hate when I have to tell people sorry.

"And I do hope you love this baby," Mommy says. "I have no idea what it's like to be the oldest in a family, but I do know what it's like to not have a sibling. It's very lonely. I bet if you think really hard, you can probably think of a time you were happy to have Dion."

I shrug.

"Like the other day when Dion played Barbies with you," Daddy says.

"Or how about when Mommy taught you how to put a ponytail in Phoebe's hair? Phoebe was so happy, she hugged you and said you were the best sister," Mommy says.

"We don't know she said that," I say. No one understands Phoebe.

"She did. Your smile was pretty big," Mommy says.

I smile too, remembering.

"Don't forget that being a big sister can be a good thing." Daddy kisses the top of my head. "We love you. Remember you can always come to us."

"Always," Mommy says, moving closer and putting her arm around Daddy and me.

"Love you too," I grumble.

"Now go and enjoy the party," Daddy says.

I stand from his lap and run, but I stop right before the door and turn. Daddy and Mommy are kissing.

Aunt Phoenix is talking with Uncle Griffin when I come up to her.

"I'm sorry, Aunt Phoenix," I say.

She bends down to my level like everyone else and tucks a strand of hair behind my ear. "Thanks for the apology, but I totally get it. Siblings are hard sometimes, but believe me, you'll be thankful when you're older."

I stare at her because I know she's wrong.

She laughs. "Go play."

I turn and run toward Dion to beat him to the game

Uncle Denver is putting together. I run faster than him and get there first, so he cries. I guess sometimes it is better being the oldest one.

11

———

Phoenix

Calista runs off to play the game Denver is organizing with water and metal bins like they're going to dive for apples at the fall fair.

"So what do you think? Ever want one?" Griffin wraps his arms around me and secures his hands on my stomach.

Griffin's older than me and he hasn't pushed, but I also don't want him to feel as though I'm the only one who gets to make the decision. We're in this together.

"Yeah." I turn in his arms. "Not that I'm not happy with Maverick."

He smiles at me and his forehead falls to mine. "I know."

I lay my arms over his shoulders, winding my fingers through his hair. "Do you want more kids?"

"With you, absolutely, but I'd like us to find some calm in the storm that is Phoenix Bailey, performer first. I don't say that because I want you to stop, but you have the tour coming up this summer. And I'd like us to enjoy traveling with Maverick first."

He's right. As strong as baby fever is in Lake Starlight these days, especially in the Bailey family, a baby will take priority over my career.

"We're going to start laying down tracks for the new album next month."

His eyes light up. "That we are."

"A baby might give us some inspiration."

"I think he or she would for sure."

"And Maverick is only getting older. More responsible," I say.

"That he is." Griffin's hands slide up my body, igniting the usual fire that burns for him.

"There's that pesky thing called a tour coming up though."

He cradles my cheeks in his palms. "I love you no matter if we have a baby next week, next year, in ten years, or never. Don't rush this on my account."

I laugh.

"I'm not some old guy, Phoenix," he says.

"I'm well aware." I waggle my eyebrows.

"Come on. Let's go bob for nipples." Griffin grabs my hand and pulls.

"Okay, but let's play our own version at home later."

He pulls me to him and my hands land on his hard chest. "You don't have to ask me twice."

Denver stops the nipple game just as we get there and announces that the dads-to-be have to play a game of stroller derby.

"Oh, this should be fun," Griffin says, finding us a place on the sidelines.

I'm standing in front of Griffin, wrapped in his arms,

while Maverick stands in front of me with my arms wrapped around him. All three of the expectant fathers stand at the starting line, their wives next to them.

Austin stretches his arms as if this race actually means something. Wyatt's back is slightly turned to Brooklyn, and Liam is lovingly hugging Savannah.

"Okay." Denver raises his hands to quiet the party, something only he can do. "The rules are simple. Your wife is going to birth the baby."

Groans commence.

"I'm kidding," he says. "The baby is in your stroller. You're going to run to the first station to put on some baby powder and a diaper. Once you finish, you strap your baby back in the stroller and run to station two, where you're going to clothe the baby, including shoes." Denver wickedly laughs. "Then you race back here and sit down to feed your baby."

Austin cracks his knuckles, and Holly kisses him on the cheek.

Savannah and Liam are practically making out, while Brooklyn and Wyatt look like a couple who got thrown together and don't really know each other. I really hope if I become pregnant, I'm more like Savannah. And yes, that's the only time you'll hear me say that.

"Everyone understand the rules?" Denver asks.

All the guys wave like, let's get on with this.

"Cleo will whistle to sound the bell," Denver says.

All three guys get in a running stance. I give my brother props for getting them to compete in this ridiculous event.

Cleo raises her hand, putting her two fingers in her mouth to whistle.

"*Stop!*" Holly steps in front of her husband.

All the rest of the Baileys move in like a swarm of bees.

Grandma Dori, even with her horrible vision, points at Cleo's hand.

Cleo lowers her hand and looks at Denver. The ring is on her right hand, so maybe it's a promise ring? I really hope that at this stage of their relationship, Denver wasn't a complete tool and got her a promise ring instead of an engagement ring.

"We're engaged!" Denver says, and Cleo blushes.

"But it's on your right hand?" I say.

Juno leaves the pack, mumbling something about weddings, and heads to the bar. Seems she's doing her best to drown her sorrows in alcohol tonight. No judgment from me. We've all been there.

"We didn't want to ruin the big day for the moms-to-be." Cleo slides it off her right ring finger and onto her left. "I had it turned around so it only looked like a band, but it keeps twirling."

Grandma Dori goes to hug them, and Denver clearly assumes he'll be first, but she passes his open arms, moving right to Cleo. The crowd laughs and Denver gives everyone an expression that makes them laugh harder.

"We're so happy for you," Holly says. "This isn't our day. We're a family. Good news is good news no matter what." Holly shoots Harley a death glare for keeping the secret about the new baby.

I think Holly's taken it upon herself to run a support group for the poor souls who marry into the Bailey family.

After another round of hugs, Denver calls the dads-to-be back over. The three of them get ready at the starting line once more. Cleo brings her hand up to her mouth and whistles.

"*Go, Liam!*" Savannah jumps up, holding her stomach as she yells for Liam like a cheerleader.

Brooklyn claps for Wyatt. At least the pregnancy hasn't made her completely heartless.

Holly's instructing Austin what to do just like a teacher would.

Poor Liam and Wyatt. Austin's the oldest of nine, and he's changed diapers and clothed babies over the years. They're at a disadvantage for sure.

Then again, Liam missed his calling as an engineer and Wyatt has proven he has the patience of a saint dealing with Brooklyn these past nine months.

"*GOOOOO, LIIAAAMMM!*" Savannah screams.

"Slow down the rah-rahs before you break someone's eardrum," I say.

Though I have to admit her overly loud and obnoxious cheering has given Liam the lead.

"Told you it'd be Liam who'd win," Griffin whispers in my ear.

All three of the men end up on the second challenge together.

"What do they win for making fools of themselves again?" I ask.

"I guess just the title of winner," Sedona says from next to me with a shrug.

All their dolls are dressed and put back in their strollers to make their way back over to their wives.

Savannah's face is bright red and she's holding her stomach with one arm as if she fears the baby might come out.

Liam is in the lead, Austin and Wyatt only footsteps behind him.

Denver's constant play-by-play has the entire room laughing and on the edge of their seats.

Savannah's pacing around and so loud, most of the

attention has turned to her, but just as Liam is about to cross the finish line, he slips on the edge of a puddle where Savannah just stood and slides all the way into the garage door of the hangar. He hits it with a bang and we all wince.

"There's a puddle under Aunt Savannah," Maverick says.

I hug him because although he's growing up so fast, he's still a kid who has no idea what a puddle of water has to do with a pregnant woman.

"Your need to compete is ridiculous," Brooklyn says to Sav.

Liam stands. "Babe, why didn't you say anything?"

Savannah walks across the room, not waiting for him, though Liam catches up. "You won. I wasn't going to ruin that."

"I guarantee the smile on her face is because she's going to be the first out of the three to have the baby," I say.

Savannah doesn't respond, waddling to Liam's truck.

"She's going to use Mom's name as the baby's middle name," Austin grumbles.

"What?" Denver asks.

Austin shrugs. "We're both having girls. We both want to honor Mom and Dad, so we agreed whoever had their baby first could use Mom's name as her middle name."

Liam's truck peels out of the parking lot as we all stare at it—before we realize we need to follow. Chaos reigns as we scramble to arrange where the kids are going and who's going with who, and it isn't until we're all leaving that I see Colton's SUV driving away with Juno in the passenger seat.

Where the hell is his fiancée?

12

____

Savannah

One thing I love about Liam is his calmness, especially when everything around him is going to shit. It's something I gather he inherited from his father, who took care of all of the details for my parents' funeral. He talked with catering and the funeral director, positioning us where we needed to be.

So it shouldn't surprise me that my water broke and Liam nonchalantly walks me to the truck, helps me in, and drives to the hospital as though we're going to the lake for a Sunday picnic.

For some reason, I thought he'd be frantic when I went into labor. Like running around searching for my suitcase and not stopping at red lights—like this one, waiting for a family of five to cross in front of us.

"Liam?" I say, channeling his calmness.

"Yeah, babe?" His fingers tap to the beat of "Beautiful Crazy" by Luke Combs.

"I don't really want to have her in the truck."

He glances over and his hand lands on my thigh. "Faster?"

"Faster," I say.

Then he looks both ways, and after the man clears the crosswalk, Liam presses down on the gas, driving as I imagined he would.

When he pulls into the circular drive of the emergency room entrance, he leaves the truck running and comes to open my door, a little more urgency in his step but nothing too out of control. He holds me to his side as I hold my stomach and we walk into the emergency room, where he helps me into a wheelchair.

"Oh!" the nurse exclaims. "The first Bailey is here. We had bets on whether we'd see any of you tonight."

I look at her quizzically.

Another nurse comes over. "A storm is due to come in."

A male nurse joins our party. Does no one else need medical attention in Lake Starlight? "Plus, it's a full moon." He points out the window.

"Really?" Liam actually seems intrigued by this useless bit of information. "Her water broke."

The first nurse becomes giddy with excitement. Maybe she made the winning bet that it'd be me who came in today. "Let's get you admitted, then Liam can fill out the paperwork."

"Thanks, Nancy," I say, reading her name tag.

"Let me run and park the truck," Liam says and dashes back the way we came.

"Sure thing." She picks up the receiver of her phone. "Might want to bring extra chairs into the waiting room.

Savannah Bailey just came in and her water broke," she says into the phone.

She hangs up as Liam returns and leans on the nurses' desk, not at all freaked out that this is happening.

We're going to be responsible for a little person's life. All their basic needs will rest on our shoulders. How can he just stand there, smiling and conversing about dark clouds and full moons? My chest squeezes and it feels harder to get a full breath of air.

I kick Liam, and he tears himself away from the riveting conversation as if he wants to become a meteorologist or something.

"You okay?" he asks.

I lean forward and smile at the male nurse who seems to think I invited him into our conversation. "I think this is a bad idea."

Liam's forehead crinkles and he bends down to my level, his hands on my thighs. "What's a bad idea?"

"The whole baby thing. Why did we think we could do this? I change my mind."

Liam laughs, all throaty and sexy. "A little late for that." He touches my stomach. "She's coming."

"In about eighteen hours probably," the male nurse chimes in.

"Eighteen hours? My water already broke." I look at him as if he doesn't know what he's talking about.

He laughs and I wish he was closer so I could kick him in the shin. "The fact that you haven't screamed once since being here means you're still in early labor. Even after your water breaks, it can be hours before active labor begins."

Well shit. I guess I should've attended those Lamaze classes or maybe read a book. It's not too late for the book though.

"Where's my phone? Get my phone."

Liam digs into my purse and hands it to me. "Want to tell everyone you're doing okay?"

"Okay, we have a room for you, Savannah. Mike here will take you up to labor and delivery. Good luck," Nancy says.

Mike rounds the edge of the desk and releases the brakes of my wheelchair. I search for the audiobook that was one of the top ten recommended books to read before your baby is born and press Play as we get into the elevator.

"It's a little late for that," Mike says and laughs.

I shoot Liam a look to say that if he laughs, he better prepare for my retaliation.

He doesn't laugh. Smart man.

"Oh, it's never too late," Liam says.

I smile at my sweet husband.

Mike finally shuts up. Thankfully.

Fifteen minutes later, I'm in a robe and on the hospital bed with monitors on my belly. The nurse brings me in a cup of ice to suck on if I'm thirsty. Nurse Katie tells me I can't eat anything.

"I never ate at the party," I admit to Liam when she leaves the room. "Go to the vending machine and grab me a bag of chips."

"Yeah, no." He fiddles with the television remote, but the foot portion of my bed moves up.

"Hello? I'm pregnant and you're supposed to be doing everything to help me right now. I'll never survive labor without food."

He mindlessly scans through the channels. "There's nothing on."

I tear the remote out of his hand. "Candy. Bar. Now."

He smiles and his hand brushes the hair from my forehead. "Nurse Katie said no."

"Nurse Katie isn't my mom. She can't tell me what to do."

"There's a reason you can't eat." He sits on the edge of the bed, and for a moment, I think about pushing him off. "We have to listen to the nurses and doctors. You wouldn't want someone who doesn't know the first thing about business coming into Bailey Timber and dictating how things should go."

I narrow my eyes at him. "I don't like you right now."

He chuckles and kisses my cheek. "I didn't really think you'd like me very much during labor, so that's okay. I've had a lucky nine months though."

The doctor comes in. Not *my* doctor, mind you. A male doctor.

Nurse Katie lifts the stirrups and I sit up straighter on the bed, shutting my thighs.

"Where's Dr. Baldwin?" I ask.

The new doctor smiles sweetly as if he totally understands why I might not be comfortable. "Unfortunately, she was on a day trip and they got caught in the storm that's headed our way."

"And you are?" Liam asks.

He sits on his rolling chair, Nurse Katie trying to get my legs in the stirrups. "Dr. Hinkle. I'm the doctor on call."

Dr. Hinkle looks like he's fresh out of medical school. I shake my head at Liam, but he shrugs.

"There are no other doctors available?" he asks.

"How old are you?" I ask.

Nurse Katie puts her hand on my arm. "Dr. Hinkle is a great doctor. He's been here a while now and delivered a lot of babies."

Nurse Katie is probably banging Dr. Hinkle.

"Sorry, it's either me or no one." He slides closer to where my legs should be open.

Liam leaves my side and stands at the foot of the hospital bed, his arms crossed. I allow Nurse Katie to put my feet in the stirrups, and I slide to the edge of the bed.

Dr. Hinkle looks behind him at Liam.

"Just making sure there's no funny business because that's mine." Liam points between my legs.

I shake my head at him even though I'm slightly wooed that he's protective of a male doctor seeing my hoo-ha.

Dr. Hinkle looks at me, his brown eyes wide with worry. But he does the examination and is very professional, then Nurse Katie helps me get out of the stirrups.

"You have a while to go. Sit tight, sleep if you can to conserve your energy. I'll come and check on you in a bit." Dr. Hinkle turns to leave.

"What's a while?" I ask.

He circles back around. "Hours. I suggest you get some rest now."

Liam shrugs and grabs the remote attached to my bed, pulling up a chair next to me.

I am not a patient woman and I have a feeling this is going to be the longest night of my life.

13

Holly

"Look at that lightning." I point at the sky through Austin's Jeep window.

"I heard the storm might be bad. Are you sure you don't want to go home and rest?" We pull out of Lifetime Adventures along with the motorcade of Baileys.

"No. I want to be there when their daughter is born."

I've loved being pregnant with my two sisters-in-law who feel more like true sisters. There's no way I would miss this birth.

Once we've driven in silence for a minute, I say, "You can stop being sour now."

Austin looks at me. "I'm the firstborn. I should get to use Mom's name for my daughter, not Savannah."

I laugh and place my hand on this thigh. "Technically, Rome could've done it with Phoebe. It's no one's right. Just be happy that her name will live on with one of her grand-children."

He says nothing. I think this whole conversation has more to do with the fact that we've yet to agree on a name. He thinks we should go generic and I want unique.

"What about Adley?"

"What's wrong with Jessica, Heather, or Emma?"

I blow out a breath. "Nothing's wrong with them. I just want something more unique," I repeat for the hundredth time. "I think Adley Bailey is a cute name."

"Adley Bailey?" He says it out loud as though he's testing it. "They end in the same three letters."

I dig in my purse and grab the baby name book we've high-lighted our top picks in. There are no names we agree on. Not one name is highlighted green—I used yellow highlighter and he used blue. We're so compatible except when it comes to this.

"Bevan?" I ask.

"Absolutely not."

"Brinley?"

"Same reasoning as Adley. Brinley Bailey."

"I think it's sweet. I'm not sure what you expect. You need to give in."

He pulls into the hospital parking lot as raindrops land on the windshield. "I should give in to what you want?"

"I'm the one who will be torn open for her to come into this world."

I feel like a jerk using the "I'm the one giving birth" card because I witnessed Austin's guilt over his helplessness during our fertility treatments. He would've taken those shots for me if he could. He was so hesitant to inject me where I was already bruised and tender. The path to parent-hood hasn't been easy for either of us. But I'm starting to panic. I want our baby girl to have a name before she arrives in this world.

"Seriously? That's your reasoning that I should be okay naming our daughter Brinley?"

He gets out of the Jeep and I open my door, holding my stomach as I lower myself to the ground. Austin's hand wraps round my arm and helps me down.

"I don't see how we're going to come to a compromise," I say, sighing.

He reaches into the back of the truck and hands me the Lake Starlight rain jacket he wears during baseball season. "Put this on."

I put it on as the raindrops become bigger. Car after car pulls into the hospital parking lot behind us. The Baileys and their significant others all file out of their cars and make their way into the hospital.

"Did you know it was supposed to storm?" I ask Sedona, who's seemed a little down since she returned to town.

"No."

She's about as easy to talk to as Austin lately.

"I'm in first," Grandma Dori says, pushing through all of us to get to the nurses' station.

The nurse stands and speaks loudly enough that we can all hear her. "Savannah is in labor and delivery. You can go to the waiting room up there."

We all wait by the elevators, having to go up in groups. Thankfully, Austin and I don't end up on the same one. Better to allow us to cool off about this name thing.

"How are you feeling?" I ask Brooklyn.

"I'm good, but Savannah going into labor has made me anxious to have our baby. But my due date is after you guys. I think I'll be the last." She frowns.

I run my hands over my stomach. "Yeah, Dr. Baldwin told me I was probably at least another week or more out."

The elevator dings and Wyatt holds the doors open for Brooklyn and me to step through. Right as we step out, a cramp hits my stomach and I stop.

"You okay, Holly?" Brooklyn asks.

I massage my stomach and straighten my back when the cramp disappears. "Yeah, I think something might not agree with me from the shower."

"I've had horrible heartburn."

Brooklyn and I continue to talk about our ailments from pregnancy on the way to the waiting room. Grandma Dori heads to the nurses' station and is soon escorted down the hallway to Savannah's room.

The kids all circle around the toys, playing while my mom and Uncle Brian watch them. My mom can't wait for her first grandchild to be born. She's agreed to decrease her hours at the diner to watch our daughter for us once I go back to work in the fall.

Everyone finds a seat, but before I can sit, another cramp grips my stomach and I blow out a breath.

"Hols!" Austin says, at my side immediately, his hand on my back. "What's wrong?"

All eyes land on me.

"Nothing, just something I ate."

He leads me to a chair, and I sit for a few minutes before another gripping pain that's worse than any menstrual cramp I've ever felt hits me.

"I'm getting the doctor," Austin says, heading to the nurses' station.

"I'm fine." I wave him off. "I was just at the doctor. They're probably those Braxton Hicks things."

Before he returns with a nurse and a wheelchair, I've got

Phoenix on one side and Harley on the other, both of their hands gripping mine.

"I hate to tell you this, but I don't think these are Braxton Hicks," Harley says.

"We'll just check you out. No harm in that," a nurse says, helping me into a wheelchair.

An hour and a half later, sweat is pouring down my face, my legs are in stirrups, and there's some Doogie Howser lookalike between my legs.

I groan as pain rips through my belly. "I need an epidural."

"You're too far along. Come on, Holly. You're almost there," the nurse says.

My mom brushes the hair off my forehead and smiles at me. "You can do this."

Austin looks pale and his hand is clammy in mine. I'm not sure either of us thought it would happen this fast.

"One more push and your baby's head will be out," the doctor says.

I look at Austin. "I'm tired."

He bends down and kisses my cheek, gripping my hand. "One more push and you can name our daughter whatever you want. Brimey, Adley, Reighleigh. Whatever."

"It's Brinley and no." A tear slips from my eye. "I want us to agree. It has to be mutual."

"I'll name the boy when we have our second child," he says with a sweet smile, his thumb swiping at my tear. "Just one more push."

I whimper and whine, but then an incredible burning sensation between my legs steals my attention and an intense need to push comes over me. I grab my mom and Austin's hands, pushing as hard as I can.

Dr. Hinkle puts up his hand. "Give me a second."

"You're kidding, right?" I ask, looking at Austin. The urge to push is so strong.

"She can't just stop, can she?" Austin asks.

But the doctor says nothing, and I hear no sounds from the baby. Panic wells inside me. Something is horribly wrong. I knew I should've asked for an older and more experienced doctor.

"Okay, one more," he says.

Tears stream down my face as I push again, and then the most glorious sound fills the room.

Our baby girl crying.

My back falls to the bed and my eyes close.

"You're kidding me!" Grandma Dori walks into the room as if there are no restrictions here and if there are, they don't pertain to her. "I missed the whole thing while waiting on Savannah and she hasn't even had one contraction."

"Congratulations, Mommy, it's a boy." The nurse places my baby in my arms.

I stare at Austin and he stares at me.

"I'm sorry, what? Our baby is a girl," I say.

The nurse opens up the blanket, and sure enough, there's a penis. "Nope, that's definitely a boy."

"But... what?" I look at Austin.

The shock is already stripped from his face, replaced with a cocky smirk. "I guess this means I get to pick the name then."

14

———

Brooklyn

We're all sitting around waiting for news on Savannah when she comes waddling out to the waiting room in a hospital gown. "Did Holly already have the baby?"

We nod. She gives Liam a scathing look as though he has any control over when she'll have the baby.

Savannah sits next to me. "This is horrible. They have me walking, and if this doesn't work, they're inducing me because my water already broke."

We all know how competitive she is, and she would've loved the bragging rights of having her baby first. Who would have guessed that Holly would go into labor so quickly she wouldn't even have time to get an epidural?

"She deserved a fast birth," Savannah says, her head resting on my shoulder. "I'm glad it was easy for her."

"For sure," I say.

The struggle Holly and Austin had to get pregnant is a far cry from Wyatt and me saying let's go off birth control and bam, I end up pregnant right away. I'm so grateful it worked out for them.

"It's a boy, by the way, not a girl," I say.

Savannah straightens, looking surprised but pleased. "So I'm the only one giving birth to a girl this time then?"

I shake my head. "Yes, Sav, you won the 'who can have a girl' competition."

I've been a bear this entire pregnancy. So much so that I'm surprised Wyatt is still sitting next to me, reading a magazine. But these feelings overtake me, and by the time I realize what I said or did, my apologies aren't worth much.

I grab his hand. Wyatt glances over at me with surprise but squeezes it. I really did get lucky when he walked into my life—or when I hit him with a flying projectile, I should say.

Without warning, a slow leak of fluid escape between my legs. I look down, expecting a puddle similar to what Savannah had, but I don't see anything.

A bolt of lightning flashes outside, thunder sounding immediately after. Phoebe runs into Rome's arms and Dion into Harley's while Calista continues playing on Rome's phone like nothing is going on around her. Even Maverick slides closer to Griffin. This storm is a doozy.

Another leak of fluid flows out of me and I look down again, but don't see anything.

Savannah's attention shifts to me after watching all the parents tell the kids it will be okay, it's just a storm.

"What are you looking at?" she asks.

I bite my lip and stand. Sure enough, there's a wet spot on the chair.

"Are you..." Savannah says.

When I release his hand, Wyatt looks at me and follows my vision to the chair, bolting up. "Did your..."

"I think so."

"Let me go get a nurse." Wyatt leaves.

Savannah's hands go up. "You've got to be kidding me!"

So much for her calm, serene personality where nothing bothers her. The redness in her face is similar to mine these months.

"The third Bailey baby. Those full moons and storms do it every time," the nurse says, helping me into a wheelchair.

"Let's go, Liam." Savannah stands and walks fast, trying to keep up with the wheelchair. "She has to be ready to come out."

"I don't think we should run or anything," Liam says.

Our family cheers us on as we leave to find our room.

Turns out, my water has a slow leak. Unlike Savannah, my contractions come right after the doctor fully breaks my water.

"Drugs," I say to Wyatt when the pain becomes too much.

"They said he's coming soon." Wyatt pulls my hand from his shirt. "Remember Lamaze and just focus on one item."

"We left the item at home. I don't have my suitcase either. I don't care what I said before. I want the drugs." I moan as all the muscles in my stomach contract.

My husband must see how serious I am because he goes off in search of the anesthesiologist. He returns with a doctor other than the one who looks like he could be Maverick's best friend. Is it wrong that the gray around his temples makes me trust him more?

Wyatt has to wait in the hallway while I get the epidural. There was a time during the pregnancy when I wanted a natural birth, but I must've been certifiable crazy. My deepest regards to the women who choose to do it without drugs, but I don't want to be one of them.

By the time Wyatt comes back in, I'm lying back in bed and feeling a little better.

Phoenix and Sedona come in to visit me since I'm comfortable now.

"We can't find Juno," Phoenix says.

"What?"

"When we all scattered, I saw her in Colton's car, but they never got to the hospital," Phoenix continues.

"You called her?" I ask.

"Like, ten times. It's either turned off or dead because it goes right to voicemail now," Sedona says.

It's not like Juno to miss anything with our family. Even with her struggles after finding out Colton was getting married, she's been there for all of us. Planning our baby shower and coming to appointments if our other halves couldn't.

"Maybe they're hashing out the whole wedding thing. I doubt she's been open to him about her feelings," I say.

Wyatt walks in with a drink from the vending machine.

"I hope so. I worry about them," Sedona says.

Grandma Dori joins the party. "Savannah is being induced. How are you, sweetie?" She scoots Phoenix out of the way to sit on the edge of my bed.

"I'm good now. The epidural is, like, a miracle worker." I smile at Grandma Dori with what feels like the first real smile I've given all day. "Have Austin and Holly named the baby yet?"

She shakes her head. "That baby will be Baby Bailey for months knowing those two."

We all laugh.

"Now that it's a boy, do you think they'll use Timothy after Dad?" Sedona asks.

Grandma Dori shrugs. "None of you have to use their names. They're a part of the babies whether you name them after your parents or not." She grabs my hand. "I'll go check on your sister and be back."

"Thanks, Grandma," I say.

She's about to leave but stops short of the door. "Have any of you seen Juno?"

We all look at one another.

"And there's my answer." She leaves the room.

Before I can start another conversation with my sisters, the nurse comes in and checks the printout from the machine that shows when I'm contracting. "How are you feeling?"

"I'm good," I say, grabbing the cup of ice chips.

"Right now. You don't feel anything?"

I shake my head. "Should I be?"

"No. It just means you're one of the lucky ones. I'm going to grab the doctor to examine you."

Phoenix stands. "And that's our cue to leave."

Sedona and Phoenix kiss me on the cheek, wish me luck, and leave the room.

The doctor comes in, still looking like he just took his medical school exam. "Sorry, it's been crazy tonight."

They position me in the stirrups again, Wyatt grabbing my hand and staying close to my head.

"Well, I'd say you're ready," he says.

"Really? This was easy," I say to Wyatt.

The doctor and nurse laugh. "You haven't pushed yet."

"After nine months of hell, we deserve a break," Wyatt says.

As the doctor and nurse prep me to push, I take Wyatt's

face in my hands. "I'm sorry. You've been so patient and kind when I've been nothing but a pain in the ass."

He smiles. "Thank you, but I get it. You're growing a baby. I'm glad to see my Brooklyn back these last few hours."

"I love you."

He kisses me. "I love you."

"Ready?" the doctor asks, interrupting our moment together.

My eyes remain on Wyatt. "Ready to be a daddy?"

He smiles. "Yeah. You ready to be a mommy?"

"I'm scared."

"Me too. But we have each other. That's all we need."

He's right. So after one more kiss, he grabs my hand and the nurse stands on my other side. I spend the next forty-five minutes pushing until our beautiful baby boy arrives into this world just after two in the morning.

"*No!*" Grandma Dori yells, coming into the room as the nurse hands me the baby. "I missed this one too."

"Sorry," I say, beaming with a smile I feel deep down to my soul.

Our baby is here.

Grandma comes over and looks at him, kisses his forehead, and leaves. "I'm going to sit in Savannah's room until that baby comes out. I'm not missing another one."

Lance Bailey Whitmore weighs in at eight pounds and three ounces. Ten toes, ten fingers, and a cone-shaped head covered by a hat. Perfection.

15

———

Liam

Savannah is growing more impatient as the news reaches us that Brooklyn had her baby.

"I don't understand," she says.

She's beside herself and I wish I could give her a definitive answer, but the doctor says that everyone is different.

"Knock, knock," Austin says from the doorway.

"Congratulations, Daddy," I say, hugging him. "I heard you had a surprise?"

He runs a hand through his hair. "We did. Turns out Elizabeth is all yours."

"If she ever comes out. I can't be that pleasant to stay inside of." Savannah's hands run over her stomach. "Why doesn't she want to come out?"

Austin laughs and sits in the chair on the other side of

her. "You have been pretty nice during the pregnancy. I'm sure Brooklyn's boy wanted out the minute he saw light."

We all laugh.

"How is she now that the baby is out?" I ask.

He nods. "She's good. Back to herself. Lance Bailey Whitmore is the name they chose."

Savannah's chin crinkles like she's going to cry. "She honored them in her own way, huh?"

"Without fighting me about Dad's name. Yeah."

Savannah holds her hand out for his. Sometimes I forget how close they are. They were the oldest when their parents died, and they helped hold the family together. Now that they're both married and all the Bailey kids are adults and on their own, they don't get to interact with one another as much.

I excuse myself to give them time together. "I'll be right back. Scream if you think it's time."

In the hallway, I pace, not willing to go too far.

Fifteen minutes later, Austin comes out and clasps my shoulder. "Thanks. I just wanted to let her know if she really wanted Elizabeth, I wasn't going to take it away from her. On the bad side, I mentioned a name Holly liked and her eyes lit up. Sorry, man." He shakes his head and walks down the hall.

I walk back into the room. I know Savannah well enough that whatever name Austin gave her will be our daughter's name. I don't really have a name preference like Austin did. I just want a healthy baby girl. Whatever we name her will suit her, I'm sure of it. Within reason of course.

"So what's her name?" I ask, resigned.

Savannah smiles. "What do you think of Brinley Elizabeth Kelly?"

I take my wife's hand and bend down. Right before my lips touch hers, I say, "I think it's beautiful, just like her mommy."

We kiss, and I'm ready to climb into bed with her until her teeth nail my bottom lip. I mumble for her to let me go and she finally does, not before she draws blood. The metallic taste flows down my throat.

"Shit, babe, I'm into kinky, but—"

She screams and grabs her stomach.

"I guess those are the contractions," I say.

And like a snap of the fingers, the Savannah I first fell in love with reappears before my eyes.

The nurse rushes in and checks the ticker tape thing. "Finally a contraction. *Yay!*" She does a little cheer and Sav cuts her a look.

Partway through the following eight hours of labor, Savannah decides she's being tormented with a long birth because she was blessed with a great personality during pregnancy. I tell her that that isn't the case and this is all part of having a baby. I massage her back, try five different positions for her to get comfortable, and she's a trooper. Demanding, but a trooper.

The entire Bailey clan hangs out from the first contraction until our baby girl makes her debut.

Brinley Elizabeth Kelly comes into this world with a wail of a scream. I expected nothing less.

"Finally," Grandma Dori says, falling into the chair beside the bed . "I'm so tired."

"You're tired?" Savannah, who after crying that she had no energy, keeps peeking to see when they'll bring the baby over to us.

"I'm older than you," Grandma Dori says before kissing

her granddaughter's cheek. "Congratulations, sweetie." She smiles at me and leaves the room to grant us some privacy.

I've loved Savannah since I was too young to truly know what love was. I thought I couldn't love her any more than I already do, but seeing my daughter in her arms, *our* daughter, almost breaks me. There's nothing sweeter in life than being with the two women who own your whole heart.

Savannah mothered her siblings, so it's no surprise to me how nurturing she is as she rocks and soothes Brinley. I crawl into bed with them as we point out that Brinley has my eyes, Savannah's lips, and if we're lucky, my temperament. It'll make the teenage years more bearable.

ALTHOUGH IT'S eleven in the morning, you'd think it's night-time judging by how dark our hospital room is.

Savannah is asleep and Brinley is in the hospital crib that reminds me of something you'd put a pet turtle in. I try to get comfortable on the vinyl chair in the corner to no avail.

As my eyes close, Brinley whimpers. Knowing I'll never sleep on this thing, I sanitize my hands and pick up my baby girl, cradling her in my arms.

She's the most beautiful thing I've ever seen.

She yawns, and her two small fists open and close, her fingers on one hand wrapping around my finger.

"My sweet baby girl, I'm your daddy. You should know, you're so loved. Your mommy is amazing and you're lucky to have her. She's probably going to be better at giving you advice because as far as I'm concerned, you won't be dating anyone until you're at least thirty."

Her face distorts with another yawn and her eyes pop open for a moment.

"Already giving me sass, huh?"

She falls back asleep.

"One thing I promise is that I'll make sure you never want for anything."

"We can't spoil her," Savannah's groggy voice interrupts me.

I smile at my wife and look back down. "I should clarify, you'll never want for food, shelter, clothing, and especially love. You'll always be loved. Probably so much you'll feel suffocated."

Savannah gives a tired laugh.

"But once again, your mommy is right. We can't spoil you, because I won't have an asshole as a kid."

"Liam!"

I chuckle and place a gentle kiss on Brinley's forehead. "Tell Mommy you don't want to be an asshole."

"Seriously," she says.

I'm not sure we're going to get any sleep, because as I slide into bed with Savannah, we stare in awe at what we made together—a life.

She's the most beautiful baby the world has ever seen, and I'd like to see someone argue that point with me.

16

Wyatt

Brooklyn's asleep and Lance is in my arms. The nine months of Brooklyn's crankiness was worth it as I admire the faces he makes and the wrinkled skin around his wrists and fingers.

My parents are ready to travel to Lake Starlight on their private plane as soon as this storm passes. I could tell by my mom's voice on the phone that she's upset she missed the birth.

When we first found out we were having a boy, I wasn't all that excited about the idea. Throughout my upbringing, I witnessed that girls all had the opportunity to do as they wished, whereas boys had to worry about the family legacy.

My dad is better with me now, but he still wishes I'd wanted to follow in his footsteps and take over the Whitmore Hotels. Now he'll probably die in his office because he won't trust anyone to take it over. He shouldn't fool himself into thinking he would've trusted me either. I never would've done the job he wanted. We're entirely different.

"I promise you can be whatever you want, and I'll support you," I whisper to my little guy.

"I missed it all." Juno stands in the doorway. Her hair's been thrown into a ponytail, but loose strands hang in every direction and her mascara and eyeliner are smeared. She's wearing yoga pants and a flannel button-down that looks way too big for her.

"Come and meet your nephew." I stand so she can sit down.

She smiles at me. "Congratulations."

"Thanks."

When she sits, I place Lance in her arms and her smile grows. "He's so beautiful. What's his name?"

"Lance Bailey Whitmore," I say.

"Love it."

I lean against the wall and watch him wrap his fingers around her finger. She looks at me like she wants to thank me.

"Did you pass out?" I ask.

I overheard Phoenix and Sedona telling Brooklyn they didn't know where she was. I saw her leave with Colton too, but first I saw Juno throw up at the side of the building before Colton helped her into his truck.

"I might have had a lot to drink."

I've been where she is. Alcohol was my go-to when things went bad with my dad and my family before I met Brooklyn. "Want to talk about anything?"

She shakes her head. "No."

"What happened to Colton's fiancée?" I press.

Juno swallows and the smile that was plastered to her

face disappears. "She had to go into work, so she left in the middle of the party."

"And Colton took you home?"

She nods.

"You two clear anything up?"

She shrugs.

That's a no.

Just then a shadow is cast by the light coming through the doorway.

"I can't believe all three of you guys had your babies." Colton gives me a handshake and a congratulations. He's not wearing his feelings as openly as Juno, but he doesn't look much better than her.

"Holly, Brooklyn, then Savannah."

Juno chuckles softly. "Savannah must have been pissed."

"She had the hardest labor, I'll tell you that. It was, like, hours," I say.

Juno stands and hands the baby to me. "I should check on the others. Tell Brooklyn I'll come by later after I shower and don't smell like a distillery."

"I will."

I sit back down, watching Colton's hand move to the small of Juno's back. He retracts it right away. They shut the door as I hear Brooklyn stir.

"Hey, you," Brooklyn softly says. "Is he hungry?"

"No. He's sleeping. Juno and Colton were just here."

She smiles. "Oh, I missed them. Where were they?"

"They didn't say, but it looks like they both just woke up."

Her eyebrows raise.

"Yeah. You might want to quiz her when she comes back tonight."

She nods and her eyes drift shut again.

"Mommy is tired. You wore her out."

Lance doesn't move.

"Let's hope when she's pregnant again, we get nice Mommy."

I raise his arm and give him a high-five.

"I love you," I say before kissing his forehead.

I can't speak for Brooklyn, but this eternal happiness and love for someone I just met makes what we share even sweeter.

17

———

Austin

"So?" I ask Holly, staring at the piece of paper taped outside our boy's crib that reads Bailey Boy.

She hems and haws. "You can pick the boy's name if you want."

I laugh and sit on the bed with her, wrapping my arm around her and holding her to my body. "We can compromise. You good with Timothy as the middle name?"

After talking with Savannah, I feel as though both of our firstborns should honor our parents.

"Let's look at the book," I suggest.

We'd highlighted some boy names before we found out we were having a girl. Maybe there's one in there we can agree on.

I dig out her book and curl back up with her on the bed. We scan page after page of yellow and blue highlights, searching for one in green. Knowing us, we won't like it now.

"Cash?" She looks at me after seeing what I highlighted.

"Don't judge. It's strong."

"Uh-huh." She flips the page. "Crew?"

I chuckle.

"And you were on me with Reighleigh," she says.

I say nothing, grabbing the book and fanning the pages to see if I can spot one.

"What about Huck?" She never highlighted it, but I did.

"Sounds a little too outdoorsy."

Then I flip forward and the book opens to the Es. It's like one name is glowing and all the other names fade on the page because it's highlighted in green.

"Easton?" I ask.

She doesn't immediately say no.

"Easton Timothy Bailey?" I say.

Her gaze veers over to the bassinet. "I like it."

"Enough to name him that?"

She nods slowly as though she's not completely convinced.

"Are you sure?" I ask.

"Yeah, I love it. Easton Bailey."

"Sounds like a baseball name," I say with a grin.

Then something dawns on her and she tilts her head. "Austin Bailey, you did not just fool me."

I laugh and kiss her temple. "You really are a baseball coach's wife."

She took a little long on the uptake. I might've highlighted because it's a popular baseball brand, but she highlighted it for her own reasons.

"Why didn't you pick Rawlings?" she teases.

"Rawlings Bailey?" I shake my head. "Easton is better." I pick up Easton and hand him to her. "Does he look like an Easton to you?"

She laughs. "Regardless of the baseball brand, I do love the name. But you will not tell him stories that he's named after the brand."

"It's a great story to tell once he makes it to the majors."

She gives me a stern look. "You will not push him to be a baseball player."

I hold up my hands. "He can be whatever he wants." I slide in next to her, and my baby boy wraps his hand around my finger. "As long as he's happy. I'll teach him to follow his heart because your heart leads you to your dreams."

She leans back and kisses my cheek. "I love you, Austin Bailey."

Nothing could ever be better than this moment right here.

"I love you," I say, and we both look at our little boy. "You need to sleep."

"I can't stop looking at him. I still can't believe after everything we went through, that he's here with us. It was a hard road to get this little guy, but worth it a million times over," Holly says.

"That's the truth. You're not upset that he's not a girl?" I ask.

A tear leaks from her eye. "I'm so happy I keep waiting for something bad to happen."

"Oh, Holly, be happy. You deserve it after everything you did. Your body and your mind took a beating, but you kept standing back up. He's your reward. Cherish this moment."

She snuggles into my body and we watch Easton coo, yawn, hiccup, and stretch, completely amazed. Life has never been sweeter.

18

———

Nurse Katie

"The waiting room is finally cleared out," I say, locking the break room door.

"Does that mean all the Baileys have been discharged?" Dr. Hinkle tears off his scrubs.

"Sure does."

"Thank God. Tell Dr. Baldwin she owes me, like, ten favors. That grandma alone is worth five. She kept following me around." He lifts my shirt and makes quick work of my bra.

I chuckle as we fall back on the twin bed that's as comfortable as a prison cot.

"Why don't we stop talking about the Baileys now?" I say, opening my thighs to make room for him. We've got about five minutes to make this happen.

"Good idea."

A loud crash sounds as something hits the floor and we

both look over the edge of the bed to find his iPad open to Lake Starlight Buzz Wheel.

"You're really getting into this town, huh?" I say.

"There was a business card for the blog on one of their charts, so I figured I'd check it out."

My hand slides to the back of his head, and I bring his lips down to mine.

Lake Starlight Buzz Wheel

Lake Starlight is raining babies. All three of our Bailey moms-to-be have delivered healthy babies. Technically the town gained another Bailey, a Whitmore, and a Kelly. I think I speak for all of us when I say, let's hope that Kelly girl doesn't have the wild streak her father had.

Holly Bailey set a record for delivering Easton Timothy Bailey in an hour and a half. He was perfection at eight pounds five ounces and twenty-one inches long.

Brooklyn Bailey-Whitmore is reported to have said her labor was a breeze. In the early morning hours, Lance Bailey Whitmore was born. Another big baby, weighing in at eight pounds three ounces and twenty-one inches long. I think there's going to be some wrestling between Easton and Lance in the years to come.

Lastly, Savannah Bailey Kelly was the first to have her water break—which broke up the baby shower—but last to deliver. Her fiery temper didn't go unnoticed as the doctors had to eventually induce her. At nine a.m. exactly, Brinley Elizabeth Kelly came into this world. Just as beautiful as her mommy but weighing more than each of her cousins. Nine pounds eight ounces and twenty-two inches long.

I wouldn't be buying any of them newborn clothes if I were you.

All families are happy and healthy at home, and I'm thankful I'm not with them because I enjoy my sleep.

In other news, it was reported that Juno had too much to drink at the baby shower and didn't make it to the hospital until the morning after all three babies were born. Someone sent in this anonymous picture of Colton helping Juno into her place after the baby shower, and this person also swears they didn't see him leave any time soon after. So what exactly transpired after he helped her inside?

Then again, Grandma Dori was overheard talking to Juno, Kingston, and Sedona at Brewed Awakenings a few days ago, saying they're all she's got left, so maybe Juno is still on the market. Is it possible that Juno and Colton crossed the lines from best friends to something more? I suppose, but where would that leave Colton's fiancée, Brigitte?

Only time will tell.

Until next time.

xo,

Buzz Wheel

COCKAMAMIE UNICORN RAMBLINGS

Oh, how fun was that? Why did all three Bailey babies have to born at the same time? Well, we didn't want you to miss any of the births, but we also didn't want to fill the pages of another Bailey's story with their siblings HEA. Hence the idea was born for Operation Bailey Babies.

Some of you might wonder why we had Austin and Holly go through infertility because this is fiction, but we like to make our books relatable. Since Rayne went through fertility treatments, she knows firsthand how many couples struggle to conceive. It's a hard journey that involves many ups and downs. It's a real struggle to be around people who so easily conceive (ahem... Rome and Harley). And at least with her, her pregnancy came with a checklist, checking off milestones month by month until she held that baby in her arms. In her case, she had two babies in her arms when she delivered boy/girl twins at thirty-one and a half weeks weighing in at 4.6lbs and 3.12lbs That's why it was equally important that Austin and Holly got their baby too.

We love doing these small novellas where we get a glimpse of previous couples but even more importantly, our upcoming couples! Which might make you wonder what's on the horizon... We've given you a lot of hints about what the last three Baileys will have to conquer before they find their HEAs. But don't worry, we have a lot more secrets up our sleeve for Juno, Kingston and Sedona.

ANOTHER GIANT HUG to our team who if not for them, we'd never be able to finish these books!

Danielle Sanchez and the entire Wildfire Marketing Solutions!

Cassie from Joy Editing for line edits.

Ellie from My Brother's Editor for line edits.

Shawna from Behind the Writer for proofreading.

Okay Creations for the cover and branding for the entire series.

Bloggers who consistently carve out time to read, review and/or promote us.

Piper Rayne Unicorns who shout from the rooftops about our new releases and love our characters like we do.

Readers who took a chance on our book with so many choices out there.

We cannot convey how excited we are for the last three Bailey siblings to get their Happily Ever After. All three took a backseat for way too long while their siblings got all the attention, but they are ready for their time in the spotlight!

XO,

Piper & Rayne

OPERATION
bailey birthday

A NOVELLA

USA TODAY BESTSELLING AUTHOR

PIPER RAYNE

Cover Photo: Wander Aguiar Photography

Cover Design: Okay Creations

1st Line Editor: Joy Editing

2nd Line Editor: My Brother's Editor

Proofreader: Shawna Gavas, Behind The Writer

LAKE STARLIGHT BUZZ WHEEL

BUZZ WHEEL PRESS RELEASE: Rumor around town is a certain matriarch of the Bailey family is having a BIG BIRTHDAY! It's even spurred a few of the Bailey kids to return home to celebrate with their beloved great-grandmother, Dori. In fact, now that there are twenty-six Bailey great-grandchildren the event is going to be overflowing with laughter and love. Also… I heard that Piper & Rayne have been speaking to some of the kids (i.e. Calista, Maverick, Easton, Brinley and Palmer) and so we're getting some special POV's. I can't wait to report my findings the day after the party!

1

———

Easton Bailey
(Fifteen and a half years old)
Austin and Holly's Son

I'm not sure what's worse. The fact that my dad saved his old-ass Jeep for me to drive when I turn sixteen or the fact that he makes me drive our entire family to school every morning as part of my "learning to drive" experience.

"You have to stop before you turn right," he dictates from the passenger seat.

"You don't want Sheriff Miller Jr. to pull you over," Mom chimes in from the back. At least she doesn't watch my every move, waiting to correct me like Dad. "Harper, you gotta eat something."

"Kind of crazy when you think of Sheriff Miller..." Dad glances at the back seat, and he and my mom exchange creepy smiles that say they're remembering a time before my sister and I were around.

"If it wasn't for the retired Sheriff Miller's daughter we

might not all be here," my mom says and runs her hand down my dad's arm.

Harper huffs. At least she'll get out of the Jeep first since she's still in middle school. "Please stop."

"It's a great story. Are you sure you don't want to hear it again?" my mom jokes. I watch in the rearview mirror as she picks up the granola bar Harper put down on her backpack and hands it back to my sister with the look of "eat the damn thing."

Having a thirteen-year-old sister has taught me that girls her age are temperamental—you never know what mood she'll be in every morning.

"If Sheriff Miller Jr. wasn't born and his mom didn't take maternity leave from the school, your mom—"

"Wouldn't have come to Alaska and been your boss," I say. "We know."

"Principal." My dad winks at my mom behind us.

I pull into the middle school to drop off Harper. She's already unbuckling her seat belt and grabbing her bag.

"Yeah, yeah, and you two fell in love." I pull the Jeep beside the curb.

"And you should both be thankful, otherwise, you wouldn't be here." My mom sounds annoyed that we're not going gaga over their love story, but seriously, they've told it a million times.

"Here you go, brat," I say, putting the Jeep into park.

My mom says my name as if it's a scolding, but we all know she'd like to call Harper that on the daily.

"Yeah, I'm so sorry I can't drive the entire way with you, East. I mean, being Mom and Dad's chauffeur and having Mom as your principal and Dad as your science teacher. I'm super jelly." She gets out, and slams the door shut.

I ignore her and roll my eyes, putting the Jeep into drive. She'll feel my pain next year when she starts high school.

"Damn her."

I look through the rearview mirror as my dad turns to face Mom. She's holding up the granola bar. Dad snatches it from her hand and opens his door. I satisfyingly put the Jeep into park again and roll down the passenger window, so I don't miss a minute of what's gonna happen. This will be good.

"Harp!" my dad yells. He jogs down the pathway a few feet, holding up the granola bar.

A honk blares from behind us and I look in the rearview mirror to see Uncle Denver in his truck. My cousins Ryder and Rohan file out, heads tucked into their coats as if they didn't just emerge from the truck.

I shift my attention back to my dad, who's waving at my sister to leave her friend group and come over to where he's standing, but a pounding on my window startles me and I look away.

"Son, you're holding up the line." Uncle Denver tries to sound like a police officer.

Sometimes I wish Uncle Denver were my dad. He's so fun and he's always doing crazy shit. But right now, he looks tired with bags under his eyes.

My mom rolls down her window. "How are the twins?"

Aunt Cleo just had another set of twins—girls this time —and Mom and every one of my aunts can't get enough of them. Maybe because they're the youngest of the Bailey brood by five years.

"They're good. Sleep, eat, shit, repeat."

"I bet they fall asleep in your arms and their little hands wrap around your fingers. The quiet nighttime feedings when it's just you and them..." My mom's eyes roll back in her head as if she'd do anything to relive that experience.

"Amazing how warped your memory can become over time. Cleo was like you until the reality of being woken by screams and never leaving the house without a stain on her clothes set in. I will say though that the betting is fun."

"The betting?" Mom asks.

"Yeah. I grabbed Abby, and Cleo put her money on Allie."

"On what?" My mom sounds as confused as I am.

"Who will walk first. Abby is so close, and the minute she walks, Cleo owes me a—" His gaze trails back to me in the driver's seat. "Well, let's just say I win."

Mom drops the subject, but I'm not some naïve little boy. Is that what marriage is like? Having to make bets to get blow jobs?

"Denver," my dad says, climbing into the car. "Did you order the balloon bouquets?"

Uncle Denver laughs. "Relax, I got it covered."

My great-grandma's ninetieth birthday party is this weekend and we've had about a million family get-togethers to talk logistics. Great-Grandma Dori is pretty much planning the entire thing while acting as though she has no idea we're throwing the party.

"I gotta get to school," I say.

Denver laughs. "Shit, East, you got the principal wrapped around your finger. Take advantage." He laughs. "See you all later." He waves and heads back to his truck, where he climbs in and speeds off around me.

"How is it that he just never grew up?" my dad says—more to himself than us, I think.

I love my dad, but he's so serious most of the time. My mom harps on my grades and about college, and my dad keeps asking me how serious I am about baseball. It's easy to tell he doesn't want to push me too hard, but I'm sure he'd be ecstatic if I chose to pursue baseball. His shot was thrown when my grandparents died, and he returned home. Although he's adamant he regrets nothing because he has my mom and my sister and me.

I drive five more minutes and park in the back of the lot of the high school because I'm pulling up with my parents —the school's principal and science teacher, who have been found way too many times making out in closets or my dad's classroom. I get razzed about them all the damn time.

I toss the keys to my dad and bolt across the parking lot.

"Have a great day, East," Mom calls.

I lift my hand in a wave without turning around. As I'm approaching the curb, Lance pulls up in his dad's truck. Uncle Wyatt files out of the passenger side to round the truck.

"Easton!" Uncle Wyatt high fives me and luckily stops my parents from breaking the distance between us.

"The Jeep?" Lance asks, cringing.

I nod as we fall into step with each other.

"My grandma called last night," Lance says. "She's buying me a new car for my sixteenth birthday."

"Lucky bastard."

We walk into the school and I nod at a few friends. Lance's dad, my uncle Wyatt, comes from a wealthy family in Manhattan, and Lance always gets extravagant gifts for holidays and his birthday.

"Once I get my license, I'll pick you up in the morning so you don't have to drive the Jeep," he says.

He'd be easy to hate if he didn't say shit like that. I remember the time he got the new game console we'd been begging for, and he let me play first. I couldn't ask for a better cousin.

"Check out Brinley," I say nodding to our cousin putting on lip gloss at her locker mirror.

Her best friend, Kenzie, is next to her, rambling on about something.

"You think she's bringing Kenzie to Grandma's party?" Lance asks.

I punch his shoulder. "I knew you had a thing for her."

He rubs his arm as if I actually inflicted pain. Lance isn't athletic. He's more into being the school president or editor of the newspaper.

"I don't, but…"

"Not many options in a school full of our damn cousins," I say what I know he was thinking.

We go to high school with six of our cousins. Three of us are referred to as the Bailey Triplets, since we were all born within a day of each other. Although Lance's last name is actually Whitmore and Brinley's is Kelly, we're all Baileys—especially in Great-Grandma Dori's eyes.

"Hey, Phoebe." I nod at our oldest cousin who attends Lake Starlight High.

Her boyfriend, Coulter, is at her side with his arm slung over her shoulder. Uncle Rome hates Coulter, but I don't know the details of why.

The bell rings, and Lance and I say goodbye and head in different directions.

I sit in my homeroom class as Kenzie sits down next to me.

"Hey, East," she coos.

I can't tell Lance that Kenzie's been flirting with me since the start of the school year. Everyone knows he likes her—that's been clear since we were kids, and she and Brinley became best friends. So I try my best not to notice her. Not notice her long dark hair and her glossy pink lips. Not notice the way her eyes fall over my body as if she'd love to jump my bones. Not notice my body's physical reaction to her. Hell, I'm fifteen, I have no control of my body, right?

"Hey, Kenzie," I say.

"Brinley invited me to your great-grandma's party. I hope that's okay?"

I glance at her to be polite and she's smiling. "My great-grandma wants the entire town there, so I'm sure she'll be thrilled."

"And what about you? Will you be thrilled if I come?"

I groan inwardly. *Lance is my cousin. Lance is my cousin. Lance is my cousin.*

I repeat the mantra to ward off the temptation of acknowledging Kenzie's attention. It works for the moment.

2

———

Calista Bailey
(Twenty-one years old)
Rome and Harley's Eldest Daughter

After the long plane ride, my legs thank me when I stand and allow them to stretch. Coming home for a week during my senior year isn't ideal, but it's Great-Grandma Dori's ninetieth birthday. If we're not all present and accounted for, she's sure to put out a search party for any missing family member.

I take my phone off airplane mode and wait for the texts from my mom or dad to say they're waiting outside baggage claim for Dion and me. As I follow the signs to baggage claim, my phone vibrates in my pocket, but I figure I'll wait until I'm down there to check it. If I'm lucky, Dion's plane came in before mine and he's waiting at my carousel already.

I step on the escalator, rolling my head to crack my neck.

Missing class while I'm back in Alaska forced me to do extra work these past couple weeks, which meant long nights of drinking a lot of coffee and getting no sleep, so it takes me a minute to process that someone is calling my name.

"Calista Bailey," the male voice says from behind me.

My head whips around. Why would *he* be here? No way he got an invite to the party. He's not family. He's not anything other than Ethel's grandson. I slowly take in his smug expression.

"Rylan Greene, how peachy to see you." I inject as much sarcasm as I can into my voice.

He's got a duffle bag over his shoulder, and he's in track pants and a sweatshirt with Stanford University stamped on it. Smug prick. Got a full ride to play soccer when I know his grades weren't nearly as good as they should have been to attend there.

"How's UCLA?" he asks.

"Fine." I hide my bitterness that I didn't get into my first choice of Stanford. It's none of his business.

"I heard you have a pretty awesome place. Your aunt's?"

I step off the escalator. "Yeah, it's nice. I gotta go. See you around."

Searching the numbers on the baggage carousels, I spot five and head that way. Dion is nowhere to be seen, which means I'll be waiting for him. My phone dings again, so I check my messages. One is from my mom in a group chat to Dion and me.

Mom: *Sorry guys, I had to volunteer for Rhea's fall party. Something came up at the restaurant for your dad. Your Great-Grandma Dori arranged a ride for you and Dion. Can't wait to see you both. Kisses.*

I sigh and see two other messages.

Dion: *I'm waiting outside. Ready to snap a picture when you see the ride Great-Grandma arranged for us. :P*

Great-Grandma Dori: *Let's go, girly. Earl's narcolepsy gets worse as the day goes on.*

I exit my texts because I probably won't figure out what my great-grandma is up to anyway. Everyone knows when it comes to Great-Grandma Dori, don't even bother. It's usually more absurd than you'd think.

Scrolling through my emails, I slide past all the clothing store promotions and sales emails and stop on one from my econ professor. Ask me again why I chose business as a degree to pursue? She wants me to check in with her when I return to talk over my assignments and grades.

Great. I'm pretty sure I'm failing the class.

Finally, the carousel moves, and luck must be on my side because my suitcase is the second one to come out. I slide between a few bodies and yank it off, checking the name to make sure the generic black suitcase is actually mine.

Rolling it behind me, I walk out the sliding doors to the pick-up area, but I don't spot any familiar cars. I reach back to grab my cell phone out of my pocket, but my hand pauses when I spot a van with Northern Lights Retirement Center on the side.

No way. When she said Earl, I assumed she meant an Uber. Dion isn't standing outside of the van, ready to take a picture, so I'm hoping it's a coincidence. Then my blue-haired great-grandma peeks her head out of the van. Once again, I was naïve about the level of embarrassment she can conjure.

"Calista!" she hollers, waving.

Sure enough, a man, Earl, I presume, is slumped over the steering wheel.

I close my eyes and say a prayer that we arrive safely in Lake Starlight. "Happy early birthday." I wheel my suitcase to the van. "Is Dion here?"

"He's already snug and secure inside." Great-Grandma Dori takes care stepping out of the van and holds my upper arms—for balance, I think, as much as a hello. Her gaze falls down my body in examination. "You're so grown up. My first great-grandchild." Then she pulls me into her arms, her red-lipsticked lips pressing to my cheeks. "Come. Come."

I help her back into the van, lifting my suitcase behind me.

Grandma Dori nudges Earl with her fist. "Wake up. We're all here."

I finish climbing the short steps with my suitcase at my side.

"Dear, you really should put a ribbon on your bag. That's how you know which suitcase is yours," Ethel says.

I shouldn't be surprised she's here. She's Great-Grandma's sidekick. I smile politely and look at the rest of the van. My jaw tics at who I find sitting two rows down by the window. Rylan's arrogance oozes around his smirk.

A flash blinds me for a second, Dion's laugh barreling out of him a millisecond later.

"Perfect. I'm sending it to Buzz Wheel right now." Dion's happy-with-himself smile shines as he steps into the aisle with his arms wide open for me. "Sis. I missed you."

I have no time to prepare or ask questions before his big body swamps me in a bear hug. Dion got my dad's height and build, where I ended up a few inches taller than my mom but not nearly as tall as I would prefer. Height that would've made me a better soccer player and gotten me into Stanford. Good thing I'm not bitter about it.

"You could have warned me," I bite out in a whisper.

"What fun would that be?" He squeezes me tighter, lifting my feet off the floor before depositing me back down.

"Sit! Earl is on a tight schedule," Great-Grandma yells.

Dion sits down in the front row with his legs stretched out, entertaining Grandma by asking if she'd like a stripper for her birthday. She shoos him away as if she has no idea there's a party. I slide into the seat behind Dion and quickly realize my mistake when Rylan's staring at me from across the aisle.

"How come I don't get a welcome like that?" he asks.

I flip him off and he laughs.

We've been competitors for as long as I can remember. When Uncle Jamie took Rylan under his wing, jealousy hit hard. I had no trouble keeping up when Uncle Jamie pitted us against one another when we were young. But as we grew older, Rylan grew stronger and faster. My workouts felt as though they capped out and I'd reached my limit.

But not Rylan. Every time he'd come into my uncles' rec place, he was bigger, gaining inches on me like he took growth hormones. Then we both applied to Stanford and the bastard got accepted even though his grades weren't even close to as good as mine. But when you have the speed, skills, and a dick, like Rylan Greene, somehow the world opens up for you.

Staring out the window, I'm struck by the fact that they've already had a snowstorm here when it's all sunshine and tans in Los Angeles. I live in my aunt's place with my cousin Maverick. Uncle Grif, Aunt Phoenix, and Jack come down sometimes, but not nearly as often now that Jack is getting older.

"Ry, sweetie, tell Dori about your girl," Ethel says.

My gut twists and I stare out the window as though I don't care.

I feel Rylan's gaze on me, watching for a reaction, before he answers his grandma. "She's nice."

Guess that confirms he does have a girlfriend. I shouldn't care. It's not as though I like him or even find him remotely attractive.

"Nice?" Great-Grandma Dori says as if he said she was a serial killer. "Nice is boring." She rolls her eyes and gives Ethel a look like *good luck with that*.

Dion peeks over the edge of the seat and I punch the back of it, making him lose his balance. He almost falls off the edge, but the bastard catches himself.

"What about you, Dion?" Ethel asks.

He glances up from his phone.

"Girlfriend?"

Dion laughs and clears his throat. "No."

"Why not? I'm sure the girls are crazy about you in North Carolina?" Great-Grandma Dori pets his ego, and I roll my eyes internally.

"Well, yeah, but I'm not settling down."

"Dating one girl isn't a marriage license," I say.

He sits up and looks over the edge of his seat. "How about you, sis? Any guys?"

I narrow my eyes at him, and he laughs, sliding back down in his seat.

Ethel smiles warmly at me. "Yeah, Calista, what about you? I'm sure the boys must be circling you."

"More like trying to escape before she devours them like chum in the water," Rylan chimes in from across the aisle.

"Ry," Ethel scolds.

"I'm concentrating on my studies this year." I don't

mention that last year was horrible for my love life. I had three boyfriends, each one worse than the last. A cheater, a thief, and a druggie-turned-dropout. "Plus, soccer takes up a lot of time."

Rylan chuckles and I whip my head in his direction, waiting for him to continue. He holds up his hands. "Relax."

"What's so funny?"

He chuckles some more. "I just wonder how high your expectations are."

"There's nothing wrong with high expectations. Does your 'nice' girlfriend meet your expectations? Does she cater to you? Give you massages after every game? Or perform other duties that you probably don't reciprocate?"

"Gross. Do not make me picture that about Rylan. Unless we're gonna talk about a girl going down on me—" Dion stops talking when Great-Grandma Dori smacks him across the back of the head.

"Behave, both of you."

We all stare out the windows, and I catch Rylan texting. Probably his perfectly *nice* girlfriend. I can't get off this bus soon enough, so as soon as we reach Lake Starlight, I step into the aisle. Great-Grandma Dori and Ethel are talking to Earl about heading to Sunrise Bay to drop off Rylan, so he takes the opportunity to ambush me in the aisle.

"Just so you know, I *am* a reciprocator and I'm usually rewarded with my name being shouted like a plea from her lips." He winks as his hard body slides by mine.

An electric current zaps my body, concentrating between my thighs. Okay, so the guy is a little attractive, I'll give him that. But attitude changes everything, and he's got it in spades.

"Thanks, Grandma, I'll catch an Uber from here." Rylan says his goodbyes to Ethel.

Grandma Dori stops me before I can get my suitcase. She looks behind her then back at me. "Just in case there is a party for me, I don't want a stripper. Your great-grandfather would roll over in his grave having some man's thing swinging in my face."

Mayday. Mayday. I have to stop my mind from forming a visual. But nope. It's right there. Great-Grandma Dori in a chair while some stripper's dick bounces to the beat of "Pony" by Ginuwine.

"I should mention though." She looks behind her again. Dion's already off the bus and I see Dad hugging him on the sidewalk. "I like strawberry cake, but marble is my favorite. With the whipped frosting, not buttercream. And definitely none of that fondant stuff."

"Noted." I nod. "No strippers and a marble cake with whipped frosting. You know... if there's a party for you."

"Yes, don't go planning one or anything. I don't want to be any trouble."

I have no idea how she keeps a straight face.

"Okay, I'm going to say hi to Dad. Thanks for the ride."

I step off the van, and my dad smiles at me. "There's my girl."

He opens his arms for me to fall into. If only I could suck back the tears that build up the instant he's holding me, as though he's ready to take on my problems. But as I clutch the back of his jacket and he runs his hands down my back, I open my eyes.

Rylan Greene is staring at me while two tears run down my cheeks. There's no smugness or arrogance, just general concern as our eyes meet.

Damn it.

I step back and wipe my tears away. The last person I'd ever want to see me at my weakest is Rylan.

My dad takes my bag. "Come on. I made a special meal for you guys."

We follow Dad down the sidewalk to his restaurant, Terra and Mare. At the doors, I give one fleeting look over my shoulder. Sure enough, Rylan is stepping into an Uber without a look back. I stop myself from caring what he thinks because I'm clearly the furthest thing from his mind.

3

———

Evie Stone
(Nine Years Old)
Juno and Colton's Eldest Daughter

"**G**reat-Grandma is taking me to get a new dress!" I tell my brother, Mason.

"You're gonna make me die!" he yells into his microphone.

"Die? Just because I'm getting a dress?" I sit on the couch in my mom's office. It's where the video game console is because Mason is addicted. At least that's what my mom says and keeping the games in here keeps him from being able to play for too long.

"Conor!" he yells at our cousin into his microphone, and I realize he's not even listening to me.

I get up and head into the kitchen. Mom's making dinner.

"When is she gonna come?" I ask, sliding up to the breakfast bar.

Mom chops up some lettuce and puts it in a bowl. Taco Tuesday is my favorite, but I'd rather have a night alone with Great-Grandma Dori.

"She said soon. But I'd really prefer it if you two ate here and then went shopping." My mom raises her eyebrows and I think she might be asking my opinion.

I never get a choice around here. "Great-Grandma promised me Lard Have Mercy pie."

My mom walks over to the fridge and grabs the cheese while meat sizzles in the pan. "I think I should go with you. I mean, now that she's using the retirement van as her mode of transportation since Ethel lost her driver's license, I'm not sure it's safe. I could drive you two and drop you off?"

"Mom. This is special. I never get Great-Grandma all to myself."

Her shoulders fall and she blows out a breath. Her red hair, which is the same as mine, is falling loose from her ponytail. "I know. We're a big family and you never get as much attention as you want."

The garage door opens and Dad walks in before petting Goldie on the head and taking off his coat. He's got the best job in the world. He's a vet and spends his whole day around animals. I want to be like him one day.

"Daddy!" I jump off the stool and run to hug him.

He hugs me tightly and kisses the top of my head. "Hey, kiddo, I heard tonight's a special night?"

He eyes my mom with a look I don't like. It's like the time he asked me about a sleepover at my cousin Maven's, but my mom had to tell me she'd gotten sick and it was canceled. This time better not be like that.

"Yep. I'm getting a new dress for her birthday."

He crouches in front of me because my dad is tall. He towers over my mom so much he complains about his neck every time they kiss. But he still kisses her all the time. It's so gross.

"Don't mention the party. It's supposed to be a surprise." He tilts his head.

I nod.

"I'm not sure it's much of a surprise," Mom says.

"Where's Mas?" Dad asks me.

I point down the hall as though we can't all hear him screaming about his video game. Dad heads down there. A second later, Mason screams as if someone is murdering him. Dad walks out with the controller and the headset, Mason following.

"Dad, I was playing Conor! He's going to brag that he beat me," my brother whines.

"That's it for today. I had a horrible day and the last thing I want to listen to is your Bailey temper."

"I'm a Stone," Mason says.

"And a Bailey," Mom says, smiling sweetly at my dad.

"More like he's a Stone with the Bailey temper," I say and smile when Dad ruffles my hair. I reposition my headband.

"I can't believe our son gets Savannah's temper and she's got sweet Asher who helps out at the Northern Lights Retirement Center every Sunday." Dad shakes his head. "Genetics make no sense."

"If it helps, I'm not sure Savannah understands it either. I'm thinking Asher got Liam's temperament and Brinley, well, she's all—"

"Savannah," all four of us say in unison and laugh.

Brinley is nice to me. She's really pretty and always wears awesome clothes, and her lip gloss is the perfect shade. But I've heard her talk to her parents. Once, she and Aunt Savannah screamed at one another for ten minutes straight until Uncle Liam went in there. I can't imagine yelling at my mom.

The front door opens and Great-Grandma Dori walks in. "I'm here!"

Mason and I run down the hallway and attach ourselves to her legs. But not too hard because my mom warned us that Great-Grandma is pretty old now and we have to be careful not to knock her off balance.

"I see you still have a key," my dad says, gaze shifting to my mom.

"Oh, Colton, you should feel lucky. In case anything should happen, I can get inside and help where I'm needed."

My dad kisses my great-grandma on the cheek. "I know. You're always looking out for us."

Mom places the spatula down and my dad ventures into the kitchen to watch over dinner while Mom hugs Grandma hello.

"Funny how I always find you two in the kitchen," Great-Grandma says.

"I'm thinking about coming with you guys," Mom says. "I could get some work done at Brewed Awakenings while you guys shop."

My great-grandma's smile turns into a frown. I'm with her. This is our time.

She pats my mom on the shoulder. "No, we're good. I got Earl, and don't worry, I just saw the nurse give him his narcolepsy medicine."

A gurgle or some weird sound comes out of my mom and she looks over at Dad.

He says, "To be honest, Dori, we don't feel entirely comfortable with the two of you going out on your own."

"Colton Stone!" Great-Grandma says.

Mason and I step back and find chairs at the kitchen table because Great-Grandma used our dad's full name and she's got that look in her eye. The same one she used on Uncle Denver when she was holding my baby cousin Abby and he tried to tell her how to do it safely.

"I might be turning ninety, but I am not delusional. I am not senile. I am not losing my mind. I would never put your daughter, my great-granddaughter, in harm's way."

My dad's not afraid of my great-grandma normally, but he looks as though he might be now. He always says he's known her his entire life, and she's helped him succeed. That she even helped him get Mom to marry him. I can't imagine why Mom wouldn't have wanted to marry my dad. He's the best.

"With all due respect, you just said the man who will be driving you suffers from a condition where he falls asleep without warning. What do you expect us to think?" Dad asks.

Great-Grandma puts her hands on her hips. "I expect you to know that I'm handling the situation. I just told you he took his medicine. He's fine."

"Fine." My dad nods to my mom, and she disappears into her office down the hall.

"Glad we're all in agreement," Great-Grandma says and looks at me. "Get your coat so we can blow this pop stand."

I rush to the front door before anyone changes their mind.

"Pop stand?" Mason asks, sitting at the table and waiting to eat. He's probably excited to have a night with just Mom and Dad. I like those nights too.

"It's a term from way back when..." Dad doesn't finish after Great-Grandma's eyes go wide. "Hey, it's taco night." He does a little dance on his way to the table. Maybe he is afraid of Grandma.

I hop after I put on my shoes and zip up my coat. "Let's go."

Mom comes down the hallway and hands me a small purse. "We got this for you. I thought you'd love to take it with you. It's like Brinley's, right?"

"OMG, Mom!" The small navy purse lays crosswise and it's just like Brinley's. "I love it!"

"Cute," Great-Grandma says.

"Why are you getting a dress, Evie?" Mason asks from the table.

"What do you care?" He wasn't interested when I was talking about it before. Why does he care now?

"Just in case there's a party, Evie should be prepared with a very pretty dress," Great-Grandma says.

"But there—" Dad's hand covers Mason's mouth.

"Evie," Mom says and squats, opening her arms. "Have fun." She squeezes me tightly and whispers in my ear, "And if anything happens, find someone you know."

"Okay."

"You two have fun." My dad hugs Great-Grandma then me.

We walk out toward the big van and I spot Earl reading a magazine in the driver's seat. He sees us and perks up, shutting the magazine. Once we're in the van, Earl lets me decide what station to listen to as he backs up out of our driveway. I wave to my mom and dad from the window. My mom looks like she did the day I went to kindergarten.

"Can I see your purse, sweetie?" Great-Grandma asks.

I hand it to her. "It's just like Brinley's. I love it so much."

She smiles and opens it as my head bobs to the music.

"I knew it." Great-Grandma takes out a cell phone. Great-Grandma struggles a bit but opens the sliding door and throws the phone into a snow bank. "Trust me, my a... butt." She smiles at me and hands me back the purse.

My eyes are wide with confusion. If Mom and Dad got me a phone, why didn't they tell me? And why would Great-Grandma throw it away? "They got me a phone?"

"No, they put it in there to track us."

"You just threw away my phone?" Why would Great-Grandma do that?

She smiles at me. "Don't worry. It wasn't a phone for you. Besides, we don't need to be tracked, do we? We're two girls out on the town."

"Two girls and Earl," I say.

"Two girls and Earl out looking for some fun." Great-Grandma puts her arm around my shoulders and kisses my temple.

Best night this week.

4

Palmer Ferguson
(Fourteen and a half years old)
Sedona and Jamison's Oldest Child

I walk into Lard Have Mercy to find my cousin Linus already in the booth in the back. He sent me a text to meet him here, so I think something happened at school today.

When I slide into the booth across from him, he peeks up from his fries. Oh, his eyes look red-rimmed and sad. Shit, I don't know that I'm the person to make him feel better. Didn't Calista and Dion return today? Why didn't he go to them?

But I know the answer. There are so many Bailey cousins —twenty-six in all—we tend to cluster with the ones we're closest in age to. Linus and I grew up together. Although the Bailey Triplets are only a year older, right now they're sophomores and we're freshmen. Somehow, that difference feels greater this year.

He lifts his hands and signs, *Thanks for coming.*

I can read lips for the most part, but in my family, it's become second nature to sign when they're around me. I'm so grateful I have a family willing to learn sign language, especially since our family is so big. I'm the only deaf Bailey, but everyone makes an effort.

I nod. *Sure. What's up?*

She broke up with me.

I wish I were surprised, but the other thing about having twenty-six cousins is that sometimes people befriend you to get closer to one of them. It could be that Linus's ex-girlfriend, Callie, really wanted Lance or Easton. Since I don't attend Lake Starlight High, I can only guess based on what Brinley and Phoebe say.

I'm sorry. I frown so he knows I mean it.

He nods and splashes malt vinegar onto his fries. I steal one from his plate. Linus slides the plate into the middle for us to share.

Did she say why? I sign, chewing my fry.

He shrugs. *She likes me as a friend.*

I frown and he nods as though he knows what I'm thinking. Linus is tall and lanky. He's slightly awkward, although I mean that in the most loving way. It's all just hormones and puberty kicking in. Callie will surely regret this decision next year once Linus has filled out.

You don't want her anyway. She doesn't appreciate you.

His hands lift. *I knew you'd say that.*

I laugh. *Isn't that why you called me here?*

At least he smiles at that. It eases my own heartache for him.

I'm not looking for an ego boost.

Are you sure? I could tell you how hot and hunky you are.

He laughs. *You're my cousin, so you don't really count.*

Hey, I'm still a girl. And I have eyes.

He picks up another fry. *I don't know why I care, other than it's embarrassing. I have to tell the family now because I asked her to come to Great-Grandma's party.*

You did? I open my eyes wide.

He nods. *She was my girlfriend.*

This is so much more serious than I thought. Linus is the romantic one out of us. He believes in soul mates and finding "the one," whereas I'm still not sure about any of that. There's so much I want to do. I want to travel and experience living by myself. Mom is always saying I should be able to stand on my own feet before settling down. Dad jokes with her that she's trying to make sure I don't make what she always felt was a mistake in her own life. Then Mom shakes her head and Dad kisses her until she's nodding.

I thought my mom and dad were great examples of young working, but I know now about all the bumps they had along the way. Because my dad was a famous soccer star for a brief moment in time, Google isn't my friend. It helped me find out a lot that I don't think they were ready for me to know.

You're only fourteen, I sign.

Exactly. Don't you want to have your first kiss?

Did you kiss her? I cringe and I wish my dislike for her wasn't so obvious. I only met Callie once, when the weather was nice by the lake. I took Isla down there to feed the ducks and Linus and Callie were lying on a blanket like two fifty-year-olds, having a picnic. Maybe if he wanted a kiss, he should've taken her there at twilight.

He answers my question with a nod.

What was it like?

I've never kissed a boy. There's this guy, Zane, at my school for the deaf in Anchorage. He just transferred in this year from the mainstream public. But I'm not ready to share anything about him with Linus yet.

I was too scared and nervous to know. It's a blur. Maybe that's why she broke up with me.

I squeeze his forearm. *No way. How many guys could she have kissed?*

I don't even want to know. If it's a lot, then I hate to say it, but she's definitely not the girl for Linus. I always pictured him with a sweet girl. An inexperienced girl. A girl who fell for his gentle nature, because Linus is going to treat his girl-friend like a prized possession.

Anyway, I got the pictures. He slides out the packages of pictures. *Took me forever to print them.*

Linus and I are in charge of arranging the pictures in the shape of a nine and a zero for the party. We spent all last weekend scouring pictures of Great-Grandma's life.

I lean back in the booth and flip through them. I find one of her and our great-grandpa, who we never met. It's actually a picture of her ice skating and my great-grandpa watching her from afar. It's the look on his face that makes me think true love might exist.

I'm not even sure why I'm so cynical about love. Everyone I know is married to who they say is their true love. And Zane makes my stomach all fluttery like movies and books say should happen. But then I think of Great-Grandma Dori and how she's spent so much of her life without my great-grandpa, and I wonder if she prefers it that way. She's in charge of her life and doesn't let anyone tell her how she should live it.

Linus taps my hand. Stop.

What?

Stop thinking about how you never want to be tied down to someone.

Yep, that's why Linus is like no other boy. He remembers conversations we had that didn't revolve around sports, video games, or girls. He was there when I Googled my dad for the first time. When I found all the rumors and the truth they hadn't told me. My dad was arrested for drunk driving on the same day I was born—but not in Lake Starlight. He was in Scotland. Linus stood by my side when I confronted my parents. He was there when they told me everything that happened. And he sat in my room as I stared out my bedroom window, wrapping my head around the news.

He bends down so I look at him. *It exists. Look where they are now.*

I know he's right, but it doesn't change how I feel about being lied to. *Let's just do this. We have to complete this and...* I stop mid-sentence because Linus is waving his hands at me.

When I turn, I find Great-Grandma walking in with Evie. I slyly gather the pictures and put them in envelopes without them seeing.

"Linus! Palmer!" I read Great-Grandma's lips. I think she might be yelling because I see Linus cringe.

We each file out of the booth because we know what to expect. She shuffles over and hugs us into her over-perfumed blouse. At least we're both taller than her now, so our heads no longer get smashed into her chest. After she releases us, I look at a very unhappy Evie.

What's wrong? I sign.

She grabs Great-Grandma's hand and holds it tightly. "It's my night with her."

I stifle a laugh.

"We were about to go anyway," Linus says to her, still signing for me.

He shoves the pictures into his backpack and digs out his wallet to pay for the fries. Damn, I really wanted to get a pie while we were here, but I get Evie's reaction. I understand how lost you can feel in a family our size. There's only one Great-Grandma.

I kiss Great-Grandma's cheek. *See you on—see you later.*

Linus kisses our grandma's cheek. After we each say goodbye to a now-happy Evie, we walk toward the exit.

I sign to Linus, *I feel like an ass.*

He shakes his head. *We all know she knows.*

Just then, Great-Grandma must call Linus's name because he touches my forearm to stop us. He nods toward her and we turn.

She signs, *Black and white is so much nicer than color.*

I realize Linus is right, so I decide to play with her a little. *For what?*

She narrows her eyes at us, and I laugh, linking my arm through Linus's and turning us to leave before Great-Grandma throws a pie in my face. As we open the door, I plow right into a hard chest. I look up and sigh when I discover it's my dad.

He lifts his hands and I wish I could put them in cement. *Linus, give us a minute.*

Linus nods and heads around the corner to the gazebo.

Can we talk?

I shrug.

Your mother is worried. She thinks we waited too long and now you're somehow scarred for life. You're too young to realize it, but love is complicated. I handled everything wrong and I've made my amends.

I look away, but Dad takes my chin in his thumb and his forefinger, pulling my face back to meet his gaze.

It's enough, Palmer. You were eighteen months old when all this went down. I'm not sure why you think your entire life is a lie. The fact that your mother and I love one another, that we raised you in a loving home, gave you everything you wanted, seems to count for nothing to you now.

His hands move faster the madder he gets, but I'm reading his lips too.

I sign, You guys lied.

We lied by omission, and we always planned to tell you. You just beat us to it. Yeah, we probably waited too long and should have realized you'd Google me at some point, but your mother is broken, and I will not have it. Be mad at me. I'm the one who allowed her to leave.

I place my hands on his to stop him from signing. *She left you when you needed help. You let her leave when she was pregnant. What does that say about love?*

He's already shaking his head. *Love is complicated. But I will not allow your mother to be upset over this. We forgave one another a long time ago. End of story.*

I have to go work on the project for Grandma's party. I huff and cross my arms. I turn to leave, but he lightly grabs my elbow.

You need to process this and flush it. Do you hear me? I will give you until Saturday. He has his "mad Dad" face.

I say nothing, and he heads into the diner. As predicted, he's buying a pie for my mom because she's upset.

I get that this whole thing has upset her, but I'm upset too. I have no idea how to process the fact that my dad was a drunk and my mom left when she was pregnant with me. The first eighteen months of my life were spent without my father. How am I supposed to get over that?

5

———

Brinley Kelly
(Fifteen and a half years old)
Savannah and Liam's Daughter

"I was a cute baby." I'm sitting on the couch with a takeout container of orange chicken from Wok 4 You. "Maybe the slide show should be only of me."

My mom glances over from her spot on the floor, and her gaze shifts to my dad, who's on the other side of the couch by me. They share a look that says, "listen to your daughter.'"

"It'll be equal between all families," my mom says.

My dad presses Play on the slide show again and exchanges his chow fun for fried rice. Asher, my younger brother, takes the chow fun and fights with his chopsticks to get a noodle.

I do love my family. My mom is a tad too protective and demanding at times, but she makes up for it during our shopping sprees. My dad is totally laid back. Although I used to be embarrassed that he runs the only tattoo parlor in Lake Starlight, I realized as I got older that most of my friends' parents hold him in high regard. He even said he might allow me to get a tattoo before I turn eighteen, but I better be sold on the design.

Asher takes after my dad in the fact they're always doing something for someone else. Fundraisers, charity auctions, Dad letting someone use his truck. Asher likes to hang out at Great-Grandma Dori's old folks' home on Sundays, reading to the residents, playing chess, or just talking. Not sure what he could possibly have in common with an eighty-five-year-old war veteran, but he finds common ground. I love him, but I never tell him that because hello... he's my brother.

"Oh!" I hold out my chopsticks toward the screen to get my dad to stop on the picture of my grandparents, Tim and Beth Bailey, who died well before I was born. Grandma is holding one of her nine kids and Grandpa is peering over her shoulder, staring into the camera, his hands lovingly resting on his wife's shoulders.

Mom looks at my dad and they share a sad smile of sorts.

My phone vibrates in the pocket of my sweatshirt, and Mom's attention quickly shifts in my direction, her usual scowl in place when my phone rings while we're eating. I'm not sure why she's so adamant about it—she's taken multiple business calls during dinners. She just says she's running a huge company and if someone is calling her, there must be a problem that needs fixing immediately.

I silence my phone without checking the screen, although I'm ninety percent sure it's Kenzie. She wants to talk about what we're wearing to my great-grandma's ninetieth birthday party. Of course I care, but she's a little *too* worried. Even mentioned having someone else do our hair and makeup. I said half the people in attendance won't even see us through their cataracts.

She doesn't think I know, but I do. She likes my cousin Easton. Officially he's my cousin, but he's really more like a brother to me. He, Lance, and I have done everything together since we were born.

First day of pre-school. All three of us in attendance.

First day of kindergarten. All three of us in the same class because it was easier on our parents.

First soccer practice. We were all there for about five minutes. Until Easton kicked the ball, hit Lance in the head, and Lance went to sit on Aunt Brooklyn's lap. I sat down in the grass and took off my new cleats. In the end, Easton kept with soccer only until T-ball started.

Easton and Lance are close and both of them like Kenzie, which is a problem. I'm hoping Easton acts like a grown-up and doesn't act on it because it would crush Lance. In truth, Lance is too good for Kenzie. Not that Easton isn't or that Kenzie is unworthy of either of my cousins. But the girl was in love with Dion for the longest time too. She likes Easton for his reputation and the fact that he's going to be the starting pitcher and he's only a sophomore. If she knew that Lance has a trust of millions coming his way once he turns twenty-one, she'd probably like him best. But we've all been sworn to secrecy with life-threatening consequences should that info leak.

While Mom goes into the kitchen, Dad restarts the slide show. She stands in the kitchen doorway and says, "I look so young. What happened?" She looks into the mirror, pulling at the sides of her face to make the skin taut.

"You're beautiful. Stop it." My dad hands me his fried

rice and I pass him the chicken. "You know I'm way too hot to be with anyone who's not a ten."

"Ten?" Asher asks.

"You know one through ten, ten being the best," Dad says.

Mom rolls her eyes. "Seriously, let's not teach him how to rate girls."

"I think Mom's as high as infinity. Infinity plus infinity." Asher smiles his huge kiss-ass grin at my mom.

She eats it up by leaning over the table and kissing his forehead. "Thank you, Ash, but we don't rate women. Women are equal to men."

Dad lets out a playful annoyed growl like "here we go again," but I know he believes it because he's always making sure I know how to take care of myself and handle myself in any situation that might come up. He's even taken me out on his bike a few times. Well, in the parking lot of Northern Lights Retirement, but it still counts.

"Oh, stop it," Mom says and swats Dad's leg, only for him to lean forward and pucker his lips.

Oh God, they're going to kiss.

"Close your eyes, Asher," I say, shutting mine.

Since I refuse to look, all I hear are Mom's giggles and Dad's soft voice—that I thankfully cannot hear because... ew.

"You can open them," Dad says.

When I do, Mom is on his lap and his face is nuzzled into her neck as if he's going to suck her blood. I sigh and place my fried rice on the table, going to the kitchen to grab more water.

On my way back, a set of headlights shine through the front window. We all look at one another as though one of us must know who's here.

Since no one else gets up, I peek through the window and see the Northern Lights Retirement Center van. Great-Grandma eases out and shuffles to the front door. The van pulls away, which means she'll need a ride home. Excitement fills me because maybe my dad will let me drive her home with him in the car.

I open the door and she strolls past me without even a hello.

"Hello, Great-Grandma," I say, but all she does is raise her hand with her back to me.

"Where's Ethel?" my dad asks her.

She sits in my spot on the sofa and I sit in my mom's spot on the floor. Great-Grandma's gaze stops on the screen. Asher purses his lips at me from across the coffee table like "what do we say or do?"

"Looking at old pictures?" Great-Grandma asks.

Mom leans forward and presses some buttons on the laptop hooked up to the television. "Yes, the pictures you gave me when you suggested that maybe someone should make a slide show." Mom stands off Dad's lap and he groans.

As much as my parents' lovey-dovey behavior annoys me —especially when my friends are over—I do hope that whoever I end up with looks at me like my dad looks at my mom. Like he never wants to be far away from her.

"I just meant because you never know when you'd need it and I'm only getting older."

"Great-Grandma!" Asher shouts as if he's wondering how she could say that.

She pats his hand. "Don't worry, I was just at the doctor and the ticker is good." She pats her chest and we all sigh with relief.

"Are you hungry?" Mom brings Great-Grandma a plate and a fork.

"I could eat." She assesses all the chopsticks in the containers, no plates to be found.

I'm not sure why my family eats Chinese food like this, but it's always been the way. Dad says it saves on dishes. It's one of those weird things you wouldn't think my mom would go along with, but she does. Sometimes my family makes comments about how my dad changed Mom, but he always says he didn't change her, he found her hidden deep down under who she thought she was supposed to be.

"I'll use chopsticks," Great-Grandma says.

"Are you sure? Do you know how?" my mom asks.

"Savannah, pass me a pair," Great-Grandma says with no patience.

Mom hands her a set that came with the food and she pulls them apart like a pro, positions them in her fingers, and brings a piece of orange chicken to her mouth. We all watch as if she's an animal at the zoo, amazed she knows how to use chopsticks.

After she chews, she looks at each of us. "What? You all think I'm so ancient. Let me tell you about the time your grandfather took me to Hong Kong."

My mom cuddles into Dad's arms, and Asher and I focus our attention on her. For the next forty-five minutes, Great-Grandma tells us about their trip. Though I never met our great-grandfather, Great-Grandma has a way of making him so vivid that it feels as if we knew him. I wonder who will do that for her one day? Which one of my aunts or uncles will tell stories to the kids about Grandma Dori?

I quickly shake my head because just like Asher, I'd rather think she'll live forever.

"I can't believe I've never heard that story," Mom says, swiping tears after she hears how when they came home, she was pregnant with my grandfather.

Great-Grandma shrugs. "He always had this way of knowing what I needed before I did." Her jaw clenches as though she's holding back tears. "Anyway, I should go." She stands.

I get the feeling she would rather pop up off the couch, but I give her a hand to get up on her feet.

"I'll drive you back." My dad rises from the sofa and kisses my mom on the temple.

I bite my lip and stare at my dad until his attention shifts to me.

He laughs and shakes his head. "Ask your great-grandma. She might not feel safe."

"Great-Grandma, can I drive you back to Northern Lights?" I fish out my shoes because one thing about Great-Grandma is she never denies us great-grandkids.

"Of course you can. I didn't live to be almost ninety without taking any chances." She winks as I slip into my shoes.

In Mom's SUV, I drive with Great-Grandma in the front and my dad in the back. We walk her to the door of her apartment and say goodbye with hugs and kisses on the cheek.

On the way home, Dad tells me how much it feels as if she's his own grandma and how great it is to feel close to Mom's side of the family. And then he drops a bomb I'm not prepared for.

"So if Kenzie likes Easton or Lance and she's upfront with telling you, speaking as someone who was in her position once upon a time, don't tell her she can't pursue something. Because you might be lucky enough to have your best friend be like your sister-in-law someday."

His words shock me because hello, we're fifteen, and

Kenzie and I promised one another we'd go to college together.

"Okaaay." But I know I won't allow her to come between them. I park the SUV in the garage, and we exit the vehicle.

My dad puts his arm around my shoulders. "You've gotten too old, too fast."

I roll my eyes though I like it when he says that. We walk in to find Asher and Mom tucked under a blanket with awe-stricken expressions.

"What did we miss?" Dad asks.

Mom points at the television. "She left a jump drive with the pictures from their Hong Kong trip."

Dad and I sit and watch the slide show of pictures of a much younger Great-Grandma Dori and our great-grandfather. It's weird to think of the life she lived before me. Great-Grandma was my age once.

I hope one day I'm in her position, having been blessed to watch my entire family grow around me. She's been through some of the worst heartbreak anyone could imagine, but she never let it make her crumble. For that alone, I want to be like Great-Grandma Dori one day.

6

———

Maverick Thorne
(Twenty-five years old)
Griffin's Son and Phoenix's Stepson

"We're going to begin our descent into Anchorage. Please find your seats and fasten your seat belts," the pilot says over the intercom.

I move from the couch to one of the chairs in my dad's private plane. Calista was supposed to be here with us. She was going to help me announce this to my family. Make sure Phoenix and dad are okay when they hear the news. All my family knows is that I'm bringing a plus-one to Great-Grandma Dori's birthday party. They don't know who that plus-one is. But Calista flew out early because she needed to get out of Los Angeles, which I get. It's so different down there from Lake Starlight.

I'm not sure how Dad and Phoenix are able to go back and forth so easily. Of course, they spend the majority of their time in Lake Starlight since Jack reached school age and they decided they wanted to give him a "normal" childhood.

I enjoy it up here too, but the pressure to move to Silicon Valley is weighing on me. The game I'm developing is finally ready to pitch. But if I move, that means I leave Calista to stay in the LA house by herself, which I'm sure she'd manage, but I'd also have to leave Raelynn.

I smile at her sitting across from me. She's nervous and probably wishes I would've dealt with this already instead of leaving her to walk into the lion's den that will be my great-grandma's birthday party.

Raelynn is Tyler Vaughn's niece, and Tyler Vaughn is Phoenix's arch-nemesis. He screwed over my dad years ago, but Dad doesn't let that get under his skin. But Tyler and Phoenix have been at odds and pitted against each other since Phoenix came into the industry.

If I'd known who Raelynn was before I met her, maybe I wouldn't have approached her at that party. No, I definitely still would have. Something about her just drew me to her.

It took until date five before she told me her connection to Tyler. She admitted that she knew who I was from pictures. Having a dad who's a well-known music producer, a mom who's a famous Hollywood actress, and a stepmom who's a pop star, puts you in magazine pictures more often than I'd like. But I grew up in the spotlight, so I'm immune to it by now.

I squeeze Raelynn's knee. She tears her eyes from looking out the window and offers me a soft smile. But we both know it's bullshit. Right now, I just want to rip off the Band-Aid and let the words fall from my mouth, like, as soon as we meet Phoenix and Dad at the car.

The plane lands on the runway and the dusting of snow reminds me of how cold it probably is.

"So they're going to meet us right now?" Raelynn unbuckles her seat belt and watches the flight attendant prepare for the stairway to lower.

I deny the urge to look out the window for fear that Phoenix will be there. A woman I love like a mother. A woman I might crush with this announcement.

"Should be." I unbuckle my seat belt and grab her bag, handing it to her.

"It's weird. I feel like I know them already when it's all just from magazines and interviews they've done." Raelynn puts on her coat, and I see her hands shake as she attempts to zip it up.

I cover her hands and do it for her. "Relax, Rae. I'm here. I won't let them..." I shake my head from my mind going to places I know my parents wouldn't go. "This is going to shock them, but that's all. They'll deal with it."

"I wish you would've told them over the phone or Face-Time. I didn't have to come." Her head falls forward and her deep auburn hair falls like a curtain on both sides of her face.

I tuck the strands behind her ears and cup her cheeks. "It's okay. It's going to be fine. I love you."

She nods and nibbles the inside of her cheek.

"Let's just get this over with." I take her clammy hand, wishing my palm was dry and confident so I could reassure her.

"Have a great visit, Mr. Thorne," Aubrey, the flight attendant, says.

"Maverick," I say. She called me Maverick until I turned twenty-one, then suddenly I was Mr. Thorne.

She smiles but doesn't respond. "Have a great time in Lake Starlight."

Aubrey smiles at Raelynn. She'd call her Miss Vaughn if she knew her last name, but she doesn't.

We walk down the stairs, and there they are. Phoenix is holding up a huge sign that reads, *Welcome Home, Maverick* and Jack limply holds another one that says *Plus-One*. Phoenix elbows Jack to be more enthusiastic, but the kid's twelve. I'm sure he's mortified she's making him do this.

Raelynn's hand goes limp in mine, but I grip it tighter before she runs back up the stairs and begs the pilot to fly her home to Los Angeles.

My dad comes out of the SUV and tucks his phone into his pocket. The hair at his temples is grayer than when I saw him last, which was only a month ago. I'm thankful he's opted not to do plastic surgery. The last thing I would want is for him to look younger than me.

When our feet hit the pavement, Phoenix jumps up and down, dropping the sign and hugging me.

"She's so pretty," she whispers in my ear. Hopefully, she hasn't examined Raelynn closely enough to see her resemblance to Tyler.

I hug her tightly because although I saw my dad last month, it's been a little longer since I saw Phoenix. "Yes, she is."

"I'm Maverick's dad, Griffin," my dad introduces himself as if Raelynn's a moron and doesn't know who he is already.

"Hello, Mr. Thorne," she says.

He chuckles. "Please call me Griffin."

Hearing the introductions, Phoenix pulls away from me and puts out her hand to Raelynn. "And I'm Phoenix."

Raelynn stares at Phoenix like a starstruck thirteen-year-old in front of her favorite boy band member. I half expect her to break out in tears. She never told me she was a fan of Phoenix's, but then again, after the news about her uncle being Tyler Vaughn, we steered clear of any conversation about my stepmom.

Phoenix doesn't give Raelynn a chance to respond before she wraps her in a hug as if I just announced we're engaged or something. But I've never brought a woman home before.

"It's nice to meet you both," Raelynn says.

I put my hand on the small of her back. "This is my girl-friend, Raelynn."

Dad and Phoenix smile at us like creepy robots until I become uncomfortable. Now definitely isn't the time to tell them. Maybe I'll let them get to know her better first.

"Jack!" I shout and beeline over to him. I move to hug him, but I see he'd like me to do anything but that, so I fist bump him. "This is Raelynn."

"Hey," he says with a nod.

"Oh, he's just pouty because he wants to go over to Ryder and Rohan's." Phoenix puts her arm around Jack, and he circles out of it.

"Go," I say. "I was going to take Raelynn on a tour of Lake Starlight."

"That'll take all of five minutes," Jack murmurs.

"Come on. We'll drop you off on our way downtown," my dad says.

Jack finally perks up.

"I wanted to give all three of you my game anyway. Get all of your perspectives."

"What did you change?" Jack's face lights up as we pile into the SUV.

Phoenix gives me a soft smile for being able to find a

connection with my brother even though there's a thirteen-year age difference.

"Let's just pick up Ryder and Rohan and bring them over to our house so Cleo only has to worry about the twins," Phoenix says to Dad once we're pulling out of the airport.

"Are you sure? Let's remember the broken television last time they came over."

Phoenix waves off Dad's concern.

I mouth, "Broken television?" to Jack.

He snickers. "Rohan. He's got a temper."

"The Bailey temper," we all say in unison except for Raelynn, laughing right after.

"I should be thankful you're a Thorne?" Raelynn asks, humor in her tone.

"He's still a Bailey at heart." Phoenix turns in her seat and pats my knee.

She's right. It took time, but the Baileys are my family.

"So tell me about the party," I say, putting my hand on Raelynn's knee. I squeeze to say, "See, things are good."

"You know Grandma Dori, acting like she has no idea what's going on but still showing up and giving ideas to people." Dad looks at me through the rearview mirror. I catch his vision shift to where my hand is on Raelynn.

We talk about the plans that have been made for the party and the fact that it's going to be a surprise, but not really. We pull up at Uncle Denver and Aunt Cleo's house to find the Northern Lights Retirement Center van parked along the curb.

"He didn't tell me she was here," Phoenix whispers.

Great-Grandma Dori and Uncle Denver are in the garage, white bags between them. Uncle Denver's hands are up, and Great-Grandma Dori's finger is pointed at him.

"Uh-oh," Phoenix says and gets out of the SUV.

"I'm staying put for this one." Dad sits idle in the driveway.

I climb out of the car, but Raelynn shakes her head. She's shy, so I allow her the reprieve of meeting two of the Bailey's most outgoing family members.

"I'm in charge of balloon bouquets. You want to talk decorations, you're talking to the wrong person." Uncle Denver pushes a hand through his hair while also pushing a stroller with his one-year-old twins, Abigail and Allison, back and forth. "And can we just admit you know?"

Grandma Dori says, "I don't know what you're talking about."

"Hello," Phoenix says with a great big wave of both her hands.

Uncle Denver blows out a breath. "Thank you. G'Ma D just dropped off some decorations she says she found on clearance at the party store. You know, just in case one of us throws a big party one of these days." He rolls his eyes but then notices me. "Mav!"

He's one of the few people I stopped correcting when he called me Mav instead of Maverick. Over the years, it started to make me feel good rather than annoyed.

He stops moving the stroller to come to me and the girls whine. "Oh, hold up." Uncle Denver brings the stroller to me, giving me a one-arm man hug while still pushing it back and forth. "They like movement, so I'll do about anything not to stop this stroller from moving."

Rohan runs out the door with his game controller.

Ryder follows with a backpack. He waves to his dad. "We'll be at Aunt Phoenix's."

Aunt Cleo follows a minute later, and she looks not nearly as put-together as she usually does. I think she's wearing Uncle Denver's T-shirt and sweatpants. "Maverick!"

Aunt Cleo beelines over and hugs me. She smells like green beans, but I don't tell her that.

"Hey, Aunt Cleo," I say.

"Maverick?" Great-Grandma Dori finally stops talking to Phoenix and hugs me tightly. "Too tall." Her bluish hair doesn't even reach my chin now. "Where's your date?"

"What?"

She shakes her head. "Someone said something about you bringing someone home with you?"

Phoenix, Uncle Denver, and Aunt Cleo all roll their eyes at the same time. I kind of like the fact Great-Grandma Dori wants to control her party but tries not to ruin their surprise.

"She's in the SUV," I say.

"Oh." She leaves me in a whoosh, and soon the back door of the SUV is open.

Shit.

Raelynn's eyes widen and she looks over Great-Grandma Dori's head at me.

"She's sweet. Shy," Phoenix chimes in from the garage.

Great-Grandma Dori is asking a lot of questions, and before I realize what has happened, Jack's eyes widen, and his mouth falls ajar.

Dad rolls down his window. "Maverick!"

His tone is the same one he used when I was ten and I didn't tell anyone the toilet overflowed. They only knew once the water dripped into his new studio.

Rohan's head peeks out from the back of the SUV. "Maverick's girlfriend's uncle is Tyler Vaughn."

I should've been prepared for Great-Grandma Dori to pull out the information before I got a chance to tell everyone myself. Slowly, I turn at the gasp behind me, not knowing if it was Phoenix or Aunt Cleo. Hell, it might've been Uncle Denver.

That happy look on Phoenix's face has been stripped off. "Is that true, Maverick?"

I nod, wishing the ground would open up and swallow me whole.

7

———

Maven Bailey
(Ten years old)
Stella and Kingston's Eldest Daughter

"What are these called again?" I ask mom before biting into the hard oval candy.

"Jordan Almonds," Mom answers, helping Mabel tie the ribbon around the box.

Dad picks up four and puts them in a box, then he passes it to me to put on the lid and tie the ribbon. We have two assembly lines going.

I chew and swallow the sweet hard candy mixed with a nut. "I don't like them."

My dad laughs. "Yeah, I'm not a fan either."

"It's tradition," Mom says. "Did you know that your great-grandma's birthday is the same day as her wedding anniversary with your great-grandfather?" She's switching from Maisey to Mabel, helping each tie the ribbons.

Dad sees her struggling and turns his attention to Maisey for a minute.

To everyone in Lake Starlight, we're the three M's. The Bailey M's—Maven, Maisey and Mabel. Either that or we get called Kingston's kids or Stella's babies. None of the nicknames are good ones. My sisters and I are each two years apart as if our parents are the best planners in the world. Last year Dad did something and now they say there will be no more kids. I don't really know what it was, but my dad was walking around with a frozen bag of peas for a few days. Maybe they ran out of names starting with M's that they liked.

"The Jordan Almonds are a way of remembering their anniversary too..." Mom continues talking to my little sister.

Mom's eyes meet Dad's across the table. They smile at one another before continuing to fill the boxes for Great-Grandma Dori's birthday party.

"Did you hear that Maverick is back?" my dad asks, clearing his throat only speaking to my mom.

"Does this mean you'll be MIA tonight, playing his new game?" Mom chuckles. She's always laughing at Dad, even though he's not that funny.

"He's dropping me off a copy. Ryder said it's awesome. The changes he made..." Dad keeps talking about a video game that my oldest cousin, Maverick, made.

I see my mom getting bored. She doesn't play video games. I watched my dad play once, but Maisey asks a lot of questions and it gets annoying. Plus, I'd rather read than play a video game.

Dad adds, "But it's who he brought with him that's the big news."

"Who?" Mom perks up and looks at my dad.

"Tyler Vaughn's niece."

My mom's mouth falls open like my little sisters' used to when my mom would play airplane to feed them.

"Who's that?" I ask.

Dad looks at me. "The guy who sings that song in the new animated movie. What's it called?" His eyes narrow and he looks to Mom for the answer.

"That new princess movie, sweetie," she says.

"Princess Helena?" Maisey asks with excitement.

Mom nods.

"That's so cool." Maisey leans back in her seat.

Mabel slumps over the table, looking bored and obviously done helping.

"It is cool, but he and Aunt Phoenix don't get along," Dad says.

"So?" I ask.

Dad tugs on one of my braids. "Sometimes people don't like it when the people they love are with relatives of people they don't like. It's complicated."

"Why?"

He laughs. As usual when our questions trap him in a corner, he looks to my mom to save him.

"You'll understand when you're older," she says, patting Mabel to sit up. Mom whispers something.

Mabel heads to the couch, lies down, and pulls a blanket over herself.

"Why does she get out of doing this?" Maisey whines.

"Because she's only six."

"I'm only eight," Maisey whines again.

"Go," Mom says.

Maisey shoots me an expression to tease me because she's free and I'm still stuck helping. But I like it when I have Mom and Dad all to myself.

Then Dad talks about the sports place he owns with

Uncle Jamison. When he looks at me, I cringe because I can already guess what he's going to ask.

"Basketball?" His hopeful eyes take in my expression before I can respond.

Being the eldest daughter of a sports fanatic like my dad and not having one athletic bone in my body sucks. Everyone always says things about my dad and how he could've had a baseball career if he hadn't hurt his shoulder in high school. Mom always gets a sad look on her face whenever anyone talks about it.

Dad runs a youth sports center where he spends his time teaching children how to play baseball, softball, and basketball while Uncle Jamison concentrates on soccer. After my cousin Calista got a scholarship to UCLA and some other boy got one to Stanford, it made them so much busier.

"King," my mom says in that voice she uses when she's not really mad, but she's not happy either.

"You have the height and I think you'd be good at it," he says to me.

Mom sighs. She gets me in ways my dad doesn't sometimes. Dad always talks about my height as though it's a good thing, but I'm too tall for my age. The tallest in my class out of all the girls. I hate it.

"She doesn't care for sports. She's more like me. All about books and learning." Mom winks at me, sliding another finished box over to the completed stack.

"True? I should quit now?" Dad looks at me.

I want to scream for Maisey and Mabel to come back. Maisey would be raising her hand and jumping up and down for my dad to teach her basketball, and Mabel would probably just talk about something else.

I nod, not wanting to say the words that will make my

dad sad.

He tugs my braid again. He always does that when he has to think about something a little longer. "What are you reading right now?"

"*Because of Mr. Terupt*. He's a schoolteacher in the fifth grade. And…"

Dad laughs and Mom smiles.

I look between them. "What?"

"You just got so excited. As excited as I was the first time I hit a double in baseball. Go on." He smiles at me and it makes me think maybe he's not that sad after all that I don't want to play basketball.

"You get all seven kids' points of view and…" I ramble on about the book.

Dad and Mom act interested. I hope they are. It's such a good book.

"Can I borrow it after you're done?" Dad asks.

"Dad…" I roll my eyes.

"Hey." He tugs my braid. "I want to read it and find out what about this book excites you so much."

I sigh. "Okay."

"Okay," he says and passes me a box to put a ribbon around.

Our front door opens and that can only mean one person is here. Even though my dad has a huge family—like, a monstrous size—most of them knock or ring the doorbell.

"Yoo-hoo!" Great-Grandma Dori says.

Maisey gets up from her play kitchen and barrels over to the door. Mom runs into the kitchen and throws Dad a bunch of dishtowels, which he tosses over the already prepared boxes. With one swipe of his arm along the table, Dad dumps everything into a bag. Jordan Almonds spill across the floor and I fall to my knees to help my dad pick them up.

Great-Grandma walks in and Dad's able to hide his hands behind his back, but the candies are all spilling out of my hands.

"What's going on?" Great-Grandma asks.

"Nothing. Just a spill."

Grandma inspects my hands, prying my fingers open. "Jordan Almonds? I haven't seen one of these since way back when I got married."

"Want one?" I ask.

"It'll break my dentures. No one my age can eat those things. Funny, I was just bringing over these chocolate color-coded candies. Gold and white and silver." She drops the bag in her hand on the table, glancing at the pile under the dishtowels at the end of the table.

"For what?" Dad asks, dropping a handful of almonds in the trash.

"Just in case someone needed favors for something. We're such a big family, there's always something to celebrate."

Dad coughs something and my mom lightly touches his arm.

"That's sweet, Dori." Mom comes over and inspects the bags. "This is a lot though."

"There's more in the van. Earl was supposed to be right behind me." She looks back toward the front door.

Dad rolls his eyes. "I have no idea why you trust a man with a medical condition like narcolepsy to take you all around town."

"Earl is fine. He's happy to do it. And I keep an eye on his medication."

Dad stomps down the hall and out the door, Maisey following. She's a total daddy's girl.

"Dori, Kingston is right. It's not safe. That's a serious medical condition and he shouldn't be driving." Mom ushers Great-Grandma to sit down, sliding out the chair for her.

"I have great vision and I'd never put myself at risk." She pats Mom's hand. "I'm good. How is your mom?"

"I finally convinced her to close Cozy Cottage B&B. She's been having flare-ups, but all in all, the doctor says she's good. Just run down. I'm hoping it helps that she's not running the business anymore." Mom shrugs. "It was a hard decision."

"I can imagine. I remember when I finally told Savannah I was done at Bailey Timber. It's hard to let go. Your mom loved her guests and loved watching them fall in love with Lake Starlight."

Mom nods but doesn't say much. Grandma isn't happy about closing down her bed-and-breakfast and got in a huge fight with Mom over it. Maisey and I sat on the stairs, hearing Mom crying to Dad about how awful she feels, but how there's no choice. The good thing is that now Grandma comes over here and watches us once a week so Mom and Dad can have a date night.

The front door shuts. Dad walks back into the kitchen and drops two more bags on the counter. "Your driver has no idea I was in the van because he's *asleep*." He sighs, going to the fridge and grabbing a beer. "Anyone else?"

"Nah. If Earl is asleep, I might have to drive home," Great-Grandma Dori says.

The fridge door slams. "Absolutely not."

"King," Mom sighs, glancing over her shoulder at him.

He takes one sip of the beer and slides it on the counter toward the sink. "I'll drive you and Uber back."

"Can I go?" I ask.

Maisey jumps next to me with her arm in the air as if we're at school. "Me too!"

Dad looks at Mom.

"I'll follow behind," she says.

"You're all being ridiculous," Grandma Dori says.

"You're going to be ninety. Sheriff Miller took your license away before he retired. When you lost your license, you couldn't drive your Cadillac, let alone a huge van. You're planning your entire birthday party while acting like you have no idea it's happening. Eventually you're going to have to slow down." My dad sounds like when he lectures the three of us about picking up our towels and clothes off the bathroom floor or when the toothpaste is dried inside the sink.

"Kingston Bailey, I will slow down when I die." Great-Grandma stands and walks out of the house.

Dad blows out a breath and throws up his hands.

Mom stands and tucks in her chair. "It's her life." She smiles at me. "Go get your coats."

Maisey and I go into the laundry room and take our coats off the hooks where we leave everything when we get home from school. I realize that Maisey's got Mabel's, but we both stop zipping our coats when we see Mom and Dad in a tight hug, Mom's hands running down Dad's back like she does to us when we've had a bad day.

We look at one another. What are we missing?

8

____

Ryder Bailey
(Twelve years old)
Denver and Cleo's son

"I could've just stayed at Jack's," my brother whines as we enter the suit store. "He's got, like, ten suits I could borrow."

"You both need to get your own suits. Your mom put me in charge. Stop complaining." Dad walks up to Mr. Carlson, who runs the only suit store in our small town. "I need these two fitted for a suit."

"You're going to pay money for something we'll wear once?" Rohan slumps in a leather chair, putting his feet on the table and pulling out his phone.

Dad ignores him. That's how it usually goes until Rohan wears that thread so thin, then it's watch out and get as far away as you can before Dad blows. I swear it's Rohan's favorite game to play.

I'm the complete opposite of my twin brother. Mom says they figured that out when we were nine months old and Rohan started walking and I waited another two months before I took my first steps. Rohan was always in awe of the television, and I enjoyed having books read to me. I took two-hour-long naps, and Rohan only took half-hour cat naps. To me, Mom makes it sound as if I'm the best kid and Rohan's the worst, but she'll occasionally say Rohan is just like Dad and I'm more like her.

Regardless, we're mirror images of each other. Most people, except our family, can't tell us apart.

"Just get Ryder fitted. We're the same size anyway," Rohan says and doesn't even look up from his phone.

Dad gives Rohan the look. The one that says, "one more word and my size twelve foot is gonna be up your butt." But Rohan doesn't notice, crossing his ankles and continuing to tap on his phone.

"If I'm going through this, so are you," I say, sitting on the chair opposite him and looking at the suits lined up perfectly on the rack. I'm not surprised we're going all out for G'Ma D, but I am surprised she's not here to make sure she likes whatever we pick out. My dad is known as the jokester of all his siblings. I wouldn't put it past him to have us show up in powder blue ruffled leisure suits like I've seen in some movies.

"Take one for the team," Rohan says.

"I always take one for the team."

He distorts his face into a "whatever" expression. Rohan's usual look. Needless to say, we're not that close, much to my dad's disappointment.

The door opens and my dad's twin walks in with our cousin Jason. He's got his phone in his hands too. Uncle

Rome nods to Dad then puts me in a headlock and gives Rohan a noogie. It's his usual hello.

"What's up, Jas?" I say to my cousin.

He sits on the coffee table. "This blows. I was just about to pass a level on Mav's new game, and I get stuck coming here. For a suit."

"We were at Jack's. What level are you on?" Rohan tucks his phone away.

"Ten," Jason answers.

As odd as it is, we all look so similar, we could be triplets. We had a new teacher last year who was convinced we were until she found out how many Baileys live in this town. Some of them don't even have the last name Bailey, but they're Baileys just the same.

"Damn it, we're stuck at nine," Rohan says in a sulky voice.

Jason shrugs and his face has that look that says he's not telling us how to pass it. Unfortunately, with big families, there's big competition, and right now, the first person to complete Maverick's video game will have bragging rights until the end of time. Maverick is, like, a genius or something and he always gives us the new version of the game after he's tweaked something. We all play it, even our uncle Kingston.

"That damn video game," Uncle Rome says to my dad.

"Bigger news than that. The developer of the game brought a surprise guest for the party," my dad says.

"Who?"

"Tyler Vaughn's niece."

"Shut up!" Uncle Rome pushes Dad in the chest as if they're still my age.

Dad nods. "I talked to Griff and he said Phoenix is trying to be all okay with it but she's also having another lock installed on the studio because everything they've been working on is in there."

"Can't say I blame her. That guy is a snake. But for Maverick to bring her home says how serious he must be about her."

"Calista said nothing?" Dad asks.

Uncle Rome shakes his head. "That girl could never be a gossip reporter. She can keep anyone's secrets. Including her own."

Dad tilts his head as though he thinks there's more that Uncle Rome isn't saying.

"Did you hear Calista and Dion got picked up by the old people van at the airport?" Jason chimes in with his own gossip. He and his sister, Calista, are total opposites.

"Love it," Rohan says. "Better them than me."

"And guess who was also in the van?" Jason looks at me like I should be able to guess.

"Who? Ethel? No surprise there," my dad says.

"Ethel and her *grandson*." Jason's voice inflicts humor when he mentions Rylan Greene, Calista's archenemy.

"Ohhh... tell me more." Dad will probably razz Calista about it the next time he sees her.

"Nothing to tell," Uncle Rome says. "But when she got off the van right after Rylan, her face was all flushed. I've always wondered if maybe there was something more than hate between those two."

"No way. The guy's a narcissist. Calista can't date him," Rohan says. I'm surprised he'd care one way or the other.

"He backs up that cockiness with skills on the field," I say.

The guy is practically a legend around here. People say he's so similar to Uncle Jamie that he's a shoo-in to go pro after college. I prefer soccer, but Rohan is baseball through and through. I look up to see my dad and Uncle Rome looking at me.

Uncle Rome turns his attention to my dad again. "I have an inkling that things aren't going so great at UCLA. Harley says maybe she just misses home. But graduation is coming at the end of this year and I think maybe Calista's struggling with that."

Mr. Carlson comes over and claps his hands in front of himself. "Okay, boys, who's first?"

"Him." Jason and Rohan both point at me.

I shrug and stand. I'd rather get it over with anyway.

While I'm in the fitting room, I hear Mr. Carlson talking to my dad and uncle about Great-Grandma's party and how she told him that if any of her family members came in to be fitted, she'd really like them to wear a gold button-down shirt and black tie.

I figured maybe we'd get a nice pair of pants and a button-down shirt. Then I'd have the pleasure of watching Rohan pulling at the linen fabric the entire night. But a tie means nice shoes too and probably a belt. I roll my eyes when Mr. Carlson lays it all out in front of me. My brother was right. This sucks.

After changing into the designated G'Ma D approved suit, I head out to the waiting room and Jason and Rohan lift their gazes from their phones and their jaws drop.

"Never," Rohan says.

"Absolutely not," Jason says.

Our dads laugh.

"Do you want to answer to G'Ma D?" Uncle Rome asks, clapping Jason on the shoulder and shifting his gaze to the other fitting room as I stand in front of the three-way mirror.

"Dad, you can't be serious. You're going to spend the

price of a new bat on a suit I'll probably rip that night?" Rohan asks.

"You're twelve now. You can't keep wearing sneakers to events like this. And plus, you'll look good for the girls." Dad winks.

Rohan gags as if he's not into girls, but he's lying. I found Mom's magazine with women wearing lingerie stuffed into his drawer the other day. Plus, his tongue practically hangs out whenever Jasmine Killborn walks by him in the hall. Can't say I blame him.

After Mr. Carlson has stuck a bunch of pins and chalk all over the fabric, I'm finally allowed to change. He says leave the suit in the dressing room and he'll take it to be altered. He turns to Rohan, who knows it's his turn but is pretending to be distracted by his phone.

"Roh, get your ass in the dressing room," Dad says.

Rohan's eyes roll back, but he pockets his phone and heads into the last available dressing room just as Jason walks out in the same get-up as me.

"Wait, we're wearing the same exact thing?" I ask.

"Leave it to G'Ma D," Uncle Rome says. "The things she gets us to do for her."

"*I'm* doing it for her. You're not matching with Uncle Denver." Jason stands up on the raised platform so Mr. Carlson can measure him, and I disappear back into the dressing room.

The door chime rings, and I wonder who else is going to fit in this small store. I get dressed in my jeans and T-shirt, slide my feet into my Vans, and walk out to find my cousins Jack, Callum, Conor, Asher, and Mason all huddled around the small table. G'Ma D and her friend Ethel are talking to Mr. Carlson.

Jason leaves the pedestal and walks to the fitting room to

undress as Rohan comes out. He steps on the pedestal and pulls out his phone, his thumbs moving across the screen, not paying attention to much around him, which is typical.

G'Ma D takes the measuring tape from Mr. Carlson and says she doesn't want the pants to be baggy, showing him how she wants it done. Her hand keeps venturing higher and the room grows quiet until Rohan jumps off the pedestal.

"G'Ma D!" he shouts, dropping his phone and covering his junk.

We all laugh. To me, that was payback for all the shit he does—except I didn't have to dish it out myself. Dad and my uncle clap, rolling back and forth in the leather chairs.

"You just got felt up by your great-grandma!" Uncle Rome says. "Classic."

It takes Great-Grandma a few seconds before she can straighten up, but when she does, she says, "Stop laughing, you two. I used to change both your diapers, so I've seen both your penises before."

The entire room "ewws," all the boys in our family probably thinking the same thing. It's a disgusting thought that we were naked in front of her at one point in our lives, whether we remember it or not.

"You all need to grow up," she says, gesturing to the pedestal for Rohan to step back up. Thankfully for Rohan, she hands the measuring tape back to Mr. Carlson. "Remember, snug fit, not baggy."

"I'm not showing my junk," Rohan says.

G'Ma D ignores him and turns her attention to my dad and uncle. "And you two? Why are you not trying something on?"

"I have a suit," Dad says.

Uncle Rome nods. "Me too."

"Not one that looks like this." She thumbs behind her.

They both lean over to look at Rohan as though they don't remember what the suit looks like. The one with the gold button-down shirt and black tie.

"Yeah. No." Dad leans back and rests his ankle on his knee.

"Yeah. Go." She points toward the dressing rooms.

"Why are we all buying suits 'just in case'?" Uncle Rome puts up air quotes.

G'Ma D looks at Ethel as though she's losing her patience.

"Stop asking questions and go," Ethel says with the authority of a well-trained sidekick.

All of us Bailey boys watch as our dads head down the hall to the change rooms. She really does have us all wrapped around her finger.

I still don't understand why we all have to match for her birthday. What kind of party is she pretending not to be planning?

9

———

Lance Whitmore
(Fifteen and a half years old)
Brooklyn and Wyatt's Son

I walk out of my bedroom as my dad steps out of his and Mom's. We freeze, our gazes soaking in what the other is wearing. We yell in unison.

"Brook!"

"Mom!"

She walks out of the bedroom, holding a necklace and handing it to my dad. He takes it, and she holds her hair up at the back. The two of them mastered this drill long before I was ever born.

She laughs. "Sorry, but Grandma Dori wants you guys to match."

"One night," Dad murmurs to me but rolls his eyes behind my mom's back.

"Don't think I don't know what you just did." Mom lets her hair fall.

Dad presses a kiss to Mom's shoulder. It's sick seeing my parents show affection all of the time.

"I just have to do one thing before we leave." Mom lifts the hem of her dress and walks down the stairs to her office. She works more than my dad lately because her business took off once she got a deal with some well-known fragrance company.

"I'm giving you five minutes," Dad calls.

Mom giggles, disappearing into her office.

I feel like an idiot, looking like a mini-me of my dad's, as I walk in front of him down the stairs. Gizmo lies in his bed in the family room, and I ignore the pang in my chest. He's barely out of that bed lately. We all act as though he's normal and we're not surprised every morning that he's still alive.

Dad opens a bottle of water and sits on the couch, pulling out his phone. "So, how is school?"

"Fine."

He peeks up at me. "And FYI, I talked to your grandma about the car."

Dread takes over me. My dad doesn't let my grandparents from New York get me luxury items very often. My grandma said if I go to college in New York, she'll buy me a condo. They bought me a new computer for my fifteenth birthday.

"And?" I ask.

"Your mom and I have the final decision. It's not going to be some sports car. We live in Alaska, for Christ's sake. What is she thinking?"

I shrug as if I didn't tell her the exact car I'd love. It's easy to get my hopes up when my grandparents, as rich as they are, want to give me the world. But the relationship between my dad and my grandfather isn't great and not nearly as easy as our relationships with my mom's family. I don't even really know my cousins in New York because they never come out here and my dad refuses to leave Lake Starlight for holidays. Which I'm grateful for. I love my life here. That's why I'm not sure I want to go away for college, but I think even Mom would be disappointed to hear that.

My dad is still eyeing me as though he wants me to say something.

"Maybe you should have had more kids. She could've shared the wealth."

He shakes his head. "Spoiled."

"It's your fault."

There was a time when I begged my parents for a sibling. Now that I'm older, I don't mind being an only child. Easton's like my brother, and maybe we get along so well because I don't have to live with him, and we don't have to share the attention of the same set of parents.

I think my mom was so caught up in starting her business and my dad in turning Glacier Point into "the place" to stay for plush luxury in Alaska, another baby just got pushed to the back burner until they felt like they didn't want to start all over again. Plus, to this day, my dad talks about how much my mom didn't enjoy being pregnant. I guess she was pretty mean for most of that nine months.

He chuckles and tips his water bottle. "Watch yourself."

I nod. "*Mom!*" I don't want us to be late.

"Coming," she says, but we both know she's not.

"Any girls coming tonight? Kenzie?"

I'm not surprised Dad sees the Kenzie thing. I like her, but I'm not blind—she likes Easton. He thinks I don't know, but when your eyes always fall to the girl you like, you notice who her eyes are following. Hers are always on Easton. And I get it. He's a jock and I'm class president. In the social hierarchy of high schools, everyone knows where the other stands.

"I think so. With Brinley."

My dad nods. "She's cute."

"Um... no. You can't say that."

"Why not? Brinley's cute." He gulps down a sip of his water.

"Because that's like the dad and the nanny or something."

"Your aunt Phoenix was a nanny for Uncle Griffin."

My mouth hangs open. "I don't want to know that. There are certain things that happened before I was born that I'd like to be blind to."

"You youth are so touchy these days."

Mom walks in thankfully and breaks up this father-son moment. "Let's go." She squats and pets Gizmo. "We'll be back late, sweetie."

He doesn't really move, and Dad watches with sadness in his eyes. Mom's going to be a mess when Gizmo walks over the rainbow bridge to the other side.

She looks at Dad. "What?"

He holds up his hands and shakes his head. "Nothing."

We all file out of the house in silence. In my dad's truck, I buckle myself in the back seat as my phone dings.

Easton: *What are you wearing?*

I laugh because I'm thinking the same thing that happened to my dad and I just happened to Easton and Uncle Austin. And no way am I telling him I'm matching him because Easton's ballsy enough to change his clothes.

Me: *Just a suit.*

Easton: *What color is your shirt?*

My thumbs pause on my screen. Yeah, if I'm stuck matching, so is he.

Me: *A blue shirt. Red striped tie.*

Easton: *Phew. Mom mentioned that Grandma Dori wants all the boys and men to match. No way!*

Me: *You're in the clear.*

Easton: *I'm ditching the tie and jacket the minute I get there, so I don't look like a damn mini-me to my dad.*

I laugh because I thought the same thing.
"What's so funny?" Mom asks.
"Nothing."
"Always nothing," she mumbles to my dad.

WE PULL up to the front entrance of the Glacier Point banquet center. My dad added the banquet hall after he bought the place. A valet driver opens my mom's door, and I step out.

"Watch out, it's slippery," the valet says.

A slight rain earlier melted the dusting of snow we got during a cold front last week, and I'm guessing the water froze on the pavement.

Dad gives the keys to the other valet, who parks our car

in the nearest spot. I guess that's how the boss gets treated. When we're at home, I never think of my dad as anything but my dad, but when we're at Glacier Point, another part of him emerges. He becomes this broad-shouldered man with tons of confidence and power. He directs and manages his staff without ever making them feel less than. From what I can tell, his staff likes him and us. Sometimes I wonder what he was like when he was my age. But Dad always says he didn't really find himself until after he met my mom. She loved him for him and not what she expected from him.

Uncle Liam drives up right behind us, and the valet opens both rear doors of their large SUV. Out walks Aunt Savannah in a dress the same as my mom's. I glance over my shoulder, and sure enough, my mom's jaw is hanging open. Not so cool of an idea when it's on the other side, huh?

"Hey, Lance sweetie." Aunt Savannah kisses my cheek and heads over to my mom, complaining about the dress and how Grandma Dori took her dress shopping. From what I pick up, Grandma Dori took them all separately and, as usual, swindled her way into getting what she wants.

Next Brinley steps out.

"Lance. You look good in a suit, per usual." Brinley has come with my family to New York a few times because she loves to shop there, and she's like the daughter my mom chose not to have. When we're with my grandparents, we go to fancy places, fancy plays, and everything is all-around just fancy. She loves it.

"You look great, but I'm doing the math on who you're going to match."

She hugs me, a light perfume lingering around us. "I hope it's no one."

She hopes, but I bet she does.

The valet holds his hand out and Brinley turns around,

which means Kenzie came with her. Uncle Liam clasps me on the shoulder, Asher right next to him, on his way over to my parents and Aunt Savannah.

Kenzie gets out of the SUV with her long dark hair swept into some half updo and her hair curled into spirals. She's wearing a lot more makeup than normal, and her dress is strapless—meaning her boobs are pushed up with a line of cleavage that's hard not to look at.

The valet shuts the door, heading to the next car.

Kenzie takes two steps, and her feet slip.

"Kenz!" Brinley screams.

I rush forward, grabbing Kenzie's elbow and her arm to steady her. She gasps as she falls back into my arms until I right her and give her my arm until we reach the rubber matting.

"Mac, we need ice melt out here immediately. Especially with the age of the guests we're having," Dad says. "I'm not being sued for twenty hip replacements."

Uncle Liam laughs and Mom swats Dad's arm.

"Thank you so much," Kenzie says once she's secure. She looks at me and I swear we share a moment.

"You're welcome."

"Look at you, saving the day." Brinley smacks me in the chest. "A modern-day Romeo."

I shake my head as heat fills my cheeks. Kenzie doesn't say anything, and the three of us walk inside the banquet room, the massive chandeliers glistening above us. The usually white room is now decorated with gold, silver, and white, with little treasure boxes in front of each place setting. A large 9-0 display is decorated in black-and-white pictures of Great-Grandma Dori throughout the years, while a slide show plays for guests to enjoy during cocktail hour. It's as big as a wedding. Great-Grandma Dori is loved in Lake Starlight, so I'm not surprised by how many guests will be here tonight.

"It's beautiful," Mom says, covering her heart.

"Everything she wanted." Aunt Savannah leans her weight against my uncle Liam.

My cousin Rhea walks in with her sister, Calista, and Asher walks over to them. He and Rhea talk about all the matching suits and dresses. As more family members trickle in, it's clear what Great-Grandma Dori did. She matched every boy and man in the Bailey family with black tuxedos and gold shirts with black ties. Every woman in my mom's generation is wearing a champagne-colored dress, while Calista and the older girls are in silver. Rhea and the younger girls are in white, which means the three M's look like triplets instead of just siblings.

Man, Great-Grandma could give Bobbie Fisher a run for his money because she's a master chess player.

10

Rylan Greene
(Twenty-one years old)
Outsider to the Bailey family
Grandma Dori's BFF, Ethel, grandson

Walking into Glacier Point banquet center with Grandma Ethel on my arm, I give my head a shake when I see so many Baileys all dressed alike. Having had Jamison Ferguson as my soccer coach for years, I've met and talked with the majority of the Baileys at one point or another. But I scan the crowd of townspeople and Baileys, eager to spot one specific.

She's standing with a group of her younger cousins, a sea of little girls in white dresses surrounding her as though she's their queen. She sneaks them each a cake pop from the table displaying a white-and-pink tiered cake with flowers cascading down to the base and a single pink candle on top. I guess Dori opted not to have the big 9-0 on top of her cake.

"There are my friends." Grandma pats my hand. "You're good, right?"

She's already sliding her arm out before I answer. It's sad when your grandma has more friends at a party than you. Then again, it is a party for a ninety-year-old.

"I'll be great. Have a good time."

Grandma could've brought anyone to her best friend's party. Hell, she could've come by herself. Most of them came in the Northern Lights Retirement Center van. She thinks I'm blind to her efforts, but after watching her with all my half-siblings over the years, I'm on to her. No doubt Dori's a part of this too.

"Rylan!" Jamison pats me on the back, putting out his hand for a shake. "I didn't know you were coming."

His little son, Conor, stands at his side, dressed like a miniature version of him. I've known the kid since he was in his mom's belly. I hold out my fist and Conor bumps it with a smile before sneaking behind his dad's legs. He's always been shy.

"Grandma wanted me to drive her." I smile.

Jamison matches my smile with a knowing look of his own. "We've all been there."

His little girl, Isla, runs over and he sweeps her up, holding her. I fist bump her and she bumps me back, harder than her brother.

"Hey, Rylan!" Isla yells.

"Can't say I'm upset about the way it all turned out though." Jamison kisses his daughter's cheek, and she squirms to get free.

"Come on, Conor!" She grabs her brother's hand and drags him away.

Another kid in the same gold shirt and black all the Bailey boys are wearing joins them, and they head to the bar.

"So how's Stanford? What are your plans for after gradu-ation?" Jamison asks.

That's the question of the fucking year. My dad's on me, my brothers are asking, even my grandma has inquired. My older brother Xavier has tried to be a guiding force since he's been down this route with football. Soccer is a different beast than football though, especially in the States. Since I started playing in college, my body's never been so beat up. I can't imagine what going pro would be like, but what else am I gonna do? Sit behind a desk and put my degree in busi-ness to use? That sounds like a jail sentence.

"I'm not sure," I answer as honestly as I can.

Jamison has never pushed me. He sat me down my freshman year in high school and talked to me about options and where I wanted to go with the game. As cocky as it sounds, I knew I had the skill. It's either the fact my parents put me through so many camps and lessons from a young age that I had a grasp on the game, or maybe I was born with the talent. Either way, even as a freshman in high school, I had options some didn't.

But as I got older, I found myself more excited to see Calista than to actually play soccer. The times Jamison had us go one-on-one were my favorite days. Especially when I was a teenager and she'd strip off her shirt to practice in her sports bra. Those were my favorite days.

"Well, don't rush into anything. That's all I'll say." He pats me on the back. "Want to get a drink? You're legal now, right?"

I nod. "Sure."

We head to the bar, passing a few Baileys and shaking hands and exchanging hellos. It isn't until after I'm holding the beer that I remember I shouldn't be. We're in the tail end of the season with a bye week right now. I won't say anything, but I'm shocked Calista missed today's game for UCLA. She could've flown home right after and probably gotten here in time.

Someone bumps into me and I almost spill my beer all over the front of my suit. I look up.

Calista is walking by with her cousin, Jamison's oldest, Palmer. She doesn't smile, but I see her lips quirk, betraying her. "Oh, sorry."

"No problem."

They disappear into the hall by the bathrooms. Maybe it's because I'm the youngest in my family, but I love how Calista's always with her cousins and paying attention to them even though they're younger.

I step away from the bar and glance out into the hall. She's hugging her cousin while Palmer cries, Calista's hands running up and down the length of her back.

"Shit, is that Rylan Greene? Tell me my sister hasn't seen you yet."

I turn to find Dion behind me.

"She's seen me and tried to spill my beer all over me." I put out my hand, and he shakes it.

Dion's never treated me badly, despite the fact that his older sister and I have been at odds for more than a decade. In fact, I think he likes the animosity between us.

"Let's switch shirts." He moves to shrug out of his jacket. "I'll take one for the team and let my shirt get ruined."

I laugh, looking at his gold button-down shirt and black tie. "I'll take my chances."

"Damn it. Can you believe this shit show?"

We look around at all the lookalikes. I lift my wrist to check the time and see how long until Dori's supposed to make her "surprise" entrance.

"My grandma is her best friend. I can believe it." I rock back on my heels. "Plus, I had to slip the DJ the music she wants played when she arrives."

He runs his hand down his face. "Do I even want to ask?"

"'Raise your Glass' by Pink." I choke on my beer from the laugh sputtering up my throat. "I thought for sure it was going to be Dean Martin or something."

"Did you really?" Dion asks with no surprise on his face.

"Nah. I half expected 'Gin & Juice' by Snoop Dogg."

Dion spits his drink all over the floor, laughing. "I can actually imagine her doing that." He imitates Snoop Dogg with the hand in the air, moving his body to the beat of the music.

"What's so funny?" Calista joins us and crosses her arms, apparently unimpressed.

"Rylan is. Who knew he was so funny!" Dion smacks me on the back and grabs a waitress, telling her about the spill on the carpet. Not that I imagine they'll do a lot since it's barely visible.

"Dion!" Callum runs up. "Did you play Maverick's game yet?"

"Catch you guys later." Dion waves and walks farther back into the room to talk video games with Callum, Jamison's oldest son. Courtesy of the Lake Starlight Buzz Wheel, I heard their cousin Maverick was developing some video game.

I turn to Calista. "I guess that leaves us."

"I need a drink."

As she turns, a squeal erupts through the speaker and I look to the front of the room, where my grandma has the microphone. She taps it as if she's a comedian or some pop star everyone's been waiting to hear from. "She's pulling in now. Everyone hide!"

The lights go out before I can find a place to go, and the only source of light is the candles floating in the bowls on each table.

"Is this really necessary?" Calista says in a low voice.

My body buzzes at having her so near in the dark. I step closer to her when I know I shouldn't. And not because I have a girlfriend. I lied in the van from the airport. My ex and I broke up weeks ago. I just wanted to see how Calista would act if she thought there was someone in my life. Because I know how I'd feel if the roles were reversed.

My hand falls to her hip as though I have no control of my appendages. She stiffens for a moment, and I hold my breath until she sinks into my hold. Her back falls to my chest, her head on my shoulder. One thing I've always liked about Calista is her height—I won't have to bend down to kiss her.

"What are you doing?" she whispers. Her minty breath fans across my cheek. She must have turned her head to look back at me.

"I have no idea."

I break the distance and allow my lips to fall on hers, knowing the consequences. She hates me, but she can't deny me. Which will probably only make her hate me more.

I slide my tongue along the seam of her lips, and she opens, her tongue sliding into my mouth, meeting my tongue. She swivels in my hold, her arms moving around my neck, and my hands slide down her back. The kiss isn't nearly as powerful as that first one years ago—it's more like a homecoming—but the longer it lasts, the more I want to push her under the table so when the lights pop on, we're still in this bubble where no one knows anything. We're still a secret.

But sadly, we're warned before the lights pop back on.

My grandma's whispers into the microphone are an ice bucket over my piqued arousal. "She's here! Shhh. One. Two."

At three, I end the kiss and step back right when the lights turn on.

I blink and take a slug from my beer as if nothing is new.

Everyone screams surprise, and Pink's voice sounds from the speakers. Dori acts surprised, and her small great-grandchildren rush to her as if she had the entire thing choreographed. I side-eye Calista. Her hands are over the back of a chair, gripping it so hard her knuckles are white. Her back rises and falls with deep breaths. Our eyes catch for a moment and I know she's feeling what I am. She wants to leave this party and be alone with me.

"I should go say happy birthday." She walks away before I can protest.

I head to the bar to get a water because I still have to drive tonight. Beer isn't good for my training anyway. Calista's dad, Rome, sidles up next to me, ordering two drinks.

"Hey, Rylan," he says.

Anxiety ratchets up my spine over the fact that two minutes after I made out with his daughter in the dark, he's approaching me as though he can sniff out my desire for his eldest daughter. "Hi, Mr. Bailey."

He waves me off. "Rome is fine."

"Okay." I crack open my bottle of water and gulp half of it as if maybe he could somehow smell his daughter's minty breath from my mouth.

"I'm gonna get to the point. Are you the reason my daughter had tears in her eyes when she got off that van?"

My memory jogs back to days earlier when I was getting

ready to get into an Uber and saw her red-rimmed eyes. "No." I shake my head.

"You sure?"

God, I'm positive. I think. His laser-focused eyes make me question if I'm correct. I've barely interacted with Calista since high school, though she crosses my mind often.

I'm so zeroed in on him, I don't see Calista approach behind her dad.

"It wasn't him. I got kicked off the team," she says.

Well, fuck. How does a skilled player like Calista get kicked off one of the best women's teams in collegiate soccer?

I shouldn't care about the answer. I shouldn't have kissed her. Hell, I shouldn't even be here. But regardless, none of it feels wrong. Maybe it's time I confess my feelings and finally see where we land.

11

——————

Grandma Dori
(Ninety years old)
*Wife to Philip, Mother to one, Grandma to nine, Grandma-in law
to nine, Great-grandma to twenty-six.*

My great-granddaughter Mabel is straddled over my
body, her arms limp around my neck. She's fast
asleep in my lap while I look at a room filled with family
and friends, people I've been blessed to know. I love the
smell of Mabel's apple shampoo. It's a scent that pulls me
back to a time when I was the mother of a young one.

As I watch my family dance together, laugh together,
and talk together, gratitude swells inside me. Through my
ninety years, my life has taken so many twists and turns—I
have no idea how I navigated myself to this moment when
all my grandkids and their children are celebrating my life.
All present and accounted for.

I wish Tim and Beth and of course my Philip were sitting

next to me, cherishing this sight as I am. My grandchildren's resilience after they lost their parents has always amazed me. The way they preserved, came together, and moved forward into their futures. And now they're all raising amazing children of their own.

Austin ruffles Easton's hair as he leads Harper to the dance floor, where he teaches her to dance—which she surprisingly seems to enjoy. Those teen years are hard. Holly comes over and the three of them end up dancing together.

My eye catches Easton sipping his soda with Brinley next to him, the two of them staring at the dance floor. Brinley puts her arm around Easton's shoulders and lays her head on his shoulder. I follow their vision to Lance dancing with Brinley's friend, Kenzie. She laughs at something Lance says and her head falls back. Lance looks at her as though he can't imagine ever looking at something so beautiful again.

Liam takes his wife's hand away from clearing one of the tables and takes her out to the dance floor, where he spins her around like a pro. They talk with Wyatt and Brooklyn, who are enjoying the quiet of a party dwindling down.

In a corner of the room, Phoenix, Griffin, Maverick, and Raelynn are huddled together with plates of cake in their hands. They smile, and although there's no laughter, all four are heavily in conversation. Phoenix goes to grab their plates, but Raelynn collects them. After she takes them to a table, Maverick puts his arm around Phoenix and whispers something in her ear. She wipes a tear from her eye.

Palmer and Linus play a board game with the younger siblings who aren't already falling asleep. She grips his arm. His smile isn't nearly as bright as it usually is. Young heartbreak can be hard, but he'll survive.

The game is interrupted by Sedona tapping Palmer on her shoulder and signing, *Can we talk?*

They move to a table by themselves to give them the privacy they need to get it all out. Palmer will realize one day that us parents do have a life before they're born. Our children may not always agree with the decisions made, but they were ours to make. Palmer will figure it out when she finds the love of her life.

Colton swoops up Mason and takes him over to Juno on the dance floor, and all three slow dance. Eventually Mason crouches under their arms and they laugh, letting him go. Then they dance together.

Jamison is in one corner with a soccer ball, teaching Rohan a trick. The rest of the boys are huddled together on their phones, playing Maverick's game.

Kingston sits down next to me, running his hand down his daughter's back. "Want me to take her?"

"Nah, I won't be able to do this forever." I press a soft kiss into Mabel's dark hair.

"I wish you could."

My dear Kingston. My ninetieth birthday has hit him the hardest. I've tried to ignore his longing stares and worry for the past few weeks, but this conversation feels inevitable now. I reach forward, careful not to drop Mabel, and pat his hand.

"I got a good twenty years left, don't you worry." I wink, but he gives me a sad smile. "Kingston, I'm going to go sometime. We all are. But know that when I do, I've had a good life. A magnificent life. And I'm so grateful for it. It wasn't all roses, but it's been the blessing of a lifetime and filled me with more joy than you can even comprehend, to watch you and your brothers and sisters make your way in the world and create families of your own. Don't be sad for me, kiddo. I'm one of the privileged ones. I got to be here to see it all happen."

He smiles.

Lucky for both of us, Stella comes over and looks at her husband with a smile. "Kids are all taken care of. Why don't you spin your wife around the dance floor?"

He stands and I mouth a "thank you" to her. She nods. Both of us are on the same page.

"After you, Mrs. Bailey," Kingston says, his eyes lighting up as he gazes at his wife.

They walk over to a corner of the dance floor that's more secluded, and Kingston holds Stella close.

The sound of a laugh pulls my attention away from my grandson and his wife. I spot Calista and Rylan at a table by themselves. She's facing him, his leg sandwiched between hers, and her forehead falls to his shoulder as a fit of laughter comes over her. He smiles at me but concentrates back on her.

Rome and Harley come into the banquet room and stop, seeing the scene in front of them. Harley pulls Rome toward the dance floor, but he keeps looking back at his oldest daughter. I guess I'll ignore the fact that they disappeared for a half hour and Harley's hair is now matted. Some things never change.

Ethel sits down in the chair Kingston vacated. "Great party."

"Yes. Thank you. For everything over the years."

She waves me off. "We're best friends. That's how we roll." She nods toward where I was just looking—Calista and Rylan. "What do you think? Gonna work?"

"All we can do is bring them together, right?"

"Do you think they're our last?" Ethel's voice is resigned.

I laugh. "I'm not ready to hang up my cape yet, are you, Louise?"

"Never, Thelma." She squeezes my hand.

"WOO HOO!" Denver yells and raises his fist.

Everyone's attention shifts to the dance floor. He's right behind Abby as she takes her first steps. Cleo runs to the other side for Abby to walk to her, and after five steps, Abby falls into her mom's arms. Cleo kisses both cheeks, holding her up in the air, laughing and smiling.

"Who's watching my kids tonight?" Denver calls. "I won the bet and now my wife needs to pay up. Which means, I need a house without kids."

The entire room fills with laughter and it's the best sound in the world. There are sad moments in everyone's life and oftentimes you find a moment of peace, but the laughter makes life worth living.

The End

COCKAMAMIE UNICORN RAMBLINGS

When we plotted out the Bailey series, the three novellas weren't part of the original plan. But since it's hard to fit in all the happily ever afters in every book when it should center on the couple for that book, we decided to do three between each set of three. Get the whole three thing? LOL

Anyway, the wedding was easy, it would be Austin and Holly. The babies were more difficult but it was fun to make it a threesome baby shower. The Birthday was *hard*. It was always going to be Dori's birthday but we were unsure how far in the future we wanted to go. At first it was going to be her hundredth birthday, but we didn't want to make her too old and... let's just say Grandma Dori lives forever!

And then we thought it would be fun to do all the kids until we realized some of the kids would be really young. But we're glad we did it because it's nice to see the parents through their children's eyes. We hope you enjoyed it as well.

Now, time to be sappy as we wipe the tears from falling. Most of you know that a little over two years ago, we plotted this series in a hotel room during a conference. It was the first time writing a series that was more than three books long and we were terrified. What if no one liked them and readership dropped off after the first couple of books? But we never could have imagined how much this family has changed our lives. Most authors thrive when readers love of their characters and that couldn't be more true of The Baileys. With every book, it made us push boundaries with twists or turns and real drama that families go through. You adopted this family as your own and championed them to other readers. The Baileys feel real to us and we think that's true for a lot of you as well. What we're trying to say is... THANK YOU! Those two words are way too simple a way to express how much gratitude we have for you loving this family like your own.

And without our team listed below, who have made this series what it is!

Danielle Sanchez and the entire Wildfire Marketing Solutions team!

Cassie from Joy Editing for line edits.

Ellie from My Brother's Editor for line edits.

Shawna from Behind the Writer for proofreading.

Sarah from Okay Creations for the cover and branding for the entire series.

Sara from Sara Eirew Photography for the awesome picture of Sedona and Jamison.

Bloggers who consistently carve out time to read, review and/or promote us.

Our Piper Rayne Unicorns who champion this series to others with their whole hearts.

You the reader who took a chance on our book with so many choices out there!

This is not goodbye to this family... just a see you later. Although we haven't made any clear decisions yet on what the future holds for The Bailey family, we're not ready to officially say goodbye either. They will have cameos in The Greene Family series though. That is one thing we can tell you for sure.

We hope to see you in Sunrise Bay!

XO,
Piper & Rayne

ABOUT PIPER & RAYNE

Piper Rayne, or Piper and Rayne, whichever you prefer because we're not one author, we're two. Yep, you get two USA Today Bestselling authors for the price of one. Our goal is to bring you romance stories that have "Heart-warming Humor With a Side of Sizzle" (okay...you caught us, that's our tagline). A little about us... We both have kindle's full of one-clickable books. We're both married to husbands who drive us to drink. We're both chauffeurs to our kids. Most of all, we love hot heroes and quirky heroines that make us laugh, and we hope you do, too.

ALSO BY PIPER RAYNE

The Rooftop Crew

My Bestie's Ex

A Royal Mistake

The Rival Roomies

Our Star-Crossed Kiss

The Do-Over

A Co-Workers Crush

The Greenes

My Beautiful Nemesis

My Almost Ex

My Vegas Groom

The Baileys

Lessons from a One-Night Stand

Advice from a Jilted Bride

Birth of a Baby Daddy

Operation Bailey Wedding (Novella)

Falling for My Brother's Best Friend

Demise of a Self-Centered Playboy

Confessions of a Naughty Nanny

Operation Bailey Babies (Novella)

Secrets of the World's Worst Matchmaker

Winning My Best Friend's Girl

Rules for Dating your Ex

The Modern Love World
Charmed by the Bartender
Hooked by the Boxer
Mad about the Banker

The Single Dad's Club
Real Deal
Dirty Talker
Sexy Beast

Hollywood Hearts
Mister Mom
Animal Attraction
Domestic Bliss

Bedroom Games
Cold as Ice
On Thin Ice
Break the Ice
Box Set

Charity Case
Manic Monday
Afternoon Delight
Happy Hour

Blue Collar Brothers
Flirting with Fire

Crushing on the Cop

Engaged to the EMT

White Collar Brothers

Sexy Filthy Boss

Dirty Flirty Enemy

Wild Steamy Hook-up